THE LAST WORD

an insomniac anthology of contemporary canadian poetry

edited by michael holmes

INSOMNIAC PRESS

Designed by Mike O'Connor

Copy editors:
Lloyd Davis
Liz Thorpe

Canadian Cataloguing in Publication Data

Main entry under title:

The Last Word: an Insomniac anthology of Canadian poetry

Poems.
ISBN 1-895837-32-4

1. Canadian poetry (English) - 20th century.*
I. Holmes, Michael, 1966 -   .

PS8279.L37 1995   C811'.5408   C95-930202-6
PR9195.7.L37 1995

Printed and bound in Canada

Insomniac Press
378 Delaware Ave.
Toronto, Ontario, Canada, M6H 2T8

Contents

Frontier College Frontière

Frontier College is a national non-profit literacy organization, which recruits and trains volunteers to tutor children, teens and adults who want to improve their reading and writing.

Frontier College was founded by students at Queen's University in 1899. Today, it works from university campus sites in every part of Canada.

The mission of Frontier College is to organize Canadian citizens to fight poverty and to work for social justice by teaching people to read and write.

"Bugs, Snakes, and Snow" reprinted from Sweet Betsy from Pike by Stan Rogal (1992) with permission from the author and Wolsak and Wynn Publishers Ltd. "Café au Lait" and "Connect the Dots" reprinted from Connect the Dots by Nicole Markotic (1994) with permission from the author and Wolsak and Wynn Publishers Ltd. "Carrie Leigh's Hugh Hefner Haiku" reprinted from Miss Pamela's Mercy by Lynn Crosbie (1992) with permission from the author and Coach House Press. "Saturday Night Fever" reprinted from VillainElle by Lynn Crosbie (1994) with permission from the author and Coach House Press. "Dear M" and "The Illusion Did Not Last" reprinted from Scoptocratic by Nancy Shaw (1992) with permission from the author and ECW Press. "Graze" and "Special Effect" reprinted from Other Words For Grace by Margaret Christakos (1994) with permission from the author and The Mercury Press. "How Can I Tell You That the World Is Round" reprinted from Eating Glass by Maggie Helwig (1994) with permission from the author and Quarry Press. "Indian Summer" reprinted from Impromptu Feats of Balance by Michael Redhill with permission from the author and Wolsak and Wynn Publishers Ltd. "Jade," "Grain Boundaries" and "Emerald" reprinted from Crystallography by Christian Bök (1994) with permission from the author and Coach House Press. "Long Distance Every Sign," "Eating the Worm" and "The Machine Gunner" reprinted from The Ecstasy of Skeptics by Steven Heighton (1994) with permission from the author and House of Anansi Press. "Orientation #6: The Iron Chink" and "Company Town" reprinted from Company Town by Michael Turner (1991) with permission from the author and Arsenal Pulp Press Ltd. "The Pipe Organ" reprinted from Organon by Matthew Remski (1994) with permission from the author. "This Claimer" and "Dark Diaspora" reprinted from Dark Diaspora In Dub by Ahdri Zhina Mandiela (1991) with permission from the author and Sister Vision Press. Pages 33-40 from Loveruage are reprinted from Loveruage by Ashok Mathur (1994) with permission from the author and Wolsak and Wynn Publishers Ltd. "Phatic Weather" and "'Hold On To Your Bag Betty': Excursive 4" reprinted from Dwell by Jeff Derksen (1993) with permission from the author and Talonbooks. Poems from Character Weakness are reprinted from Character Weakness by Judy Radul (1993) with permission from the author. Poems from Low Fancy are reprinted from Low Fancy by Catriona Strang (1993) with permission from the author and ECW Press. "Pressure" and "A Visitor" reprinted from In The House Of Slaves by Evelyn Lau (1994) with permission from the author and Coach House Press. "Who Is Luis Possy?" reprinted from Tender Agencies by Dennis Denisoff (1994) with permission from the author and Arsenal Pulp Press Ltd.

Word to the Wise:
an introduction to The Last Word

Shortly after Dennis Lee's anthology *The New Canadian Poets: 1970-1985* was published by McClelland & Stewart I started haunting a Toronto restaurant that, for a while, held the city's only "open-mic" reading series. Ten years later, I realize that the events were (though perhaps obliquely) related. Like me, the people who ran the show could be described as young and enthusiastic writers who had little time for the generation of poets — documented, for example, in Lee's book — just beginning to establish their credentials. What we knew about the heritage or contemporary scope of Canadian poetry could fit into the beermug used to draw the names of the performers. We were brash, affected and judgmental "artists" with the conjurer's flair for the dramatic. For the most part the poetry was dreadful.

Soon I found myself hosting the readings. I made a few great lifelong friends because of it, despite a growing dissatisfaction with what I quickly realized was a general tendency to prioritize and celebrate the magician's patter and pyrotechnics of performance over anything that could be described as captivating, innovative, or beautiful poetry. For my money, the best thing about those sometimes tedious, sometimes glorious Thursday nights was that we started to make a point of challenging people to actually *read* poetry. To, as *Public Enemy* might say, "learn your culture." We asked them to buy another writer's book and perform a "cover" poem — to treat somebody's poem like a song you've always wanted to sing. In my mind it was the world's first poetry karaoke bar ... featuring so-and-so doing Nichol or Dewdney or Marlatt or Atwood.

You see, on occasion I imagine Canada a nation of 30 million poets. What disturbs me is how few of them will ever consider purchasing a book of poetry.

After eight years our reading series eventually died. No big loss — there were few who mourned: other people were, and are (for now), simply, more committed to organizing public "literary" performances. In Toronto, during the mid-80s, we were just about the only game in town. By the mid-90s poetry (and what's become known as "The Spoken Word") had become "hip": the flavour of the month.

At present, you can go to a reading on almost any given night of any week. It doesn't matter whether you're in Vancouver or Calgary or Montréal or Halifax — something's probably happening. Smaller towns and cities have their regular events too — in cafés and bars, under tents, on hilltops — wherever. And sometimes the experience will be worthwhile, *truly* magical. In fact, a couple of those brash folks I first met years ago actually took the time to learn their craft and become, in my opinion, important poets. Along the way I've been fortunate enough to have met and read the work of others who have been just as spellbinding and inspirational. A number of them are what I would call *compelling*, even *brilliant*, performers of their own writing.

All of them, however, have one thing in common (I can't believe I'm about to write this, but the sad truth is that the point must be made): their poetry "works" *because of* — not despite — the words *printed* on the page.

In the coming months some people will try to convince you that there's currently a "populist push" rejuvenating contemporary literature. They'll argue that "slams," "open-mics," and corporate sponsorship are indicators of interest in an exciting "new wave" of young, street-wise writers. They may not, however, be telling you the whole truth. In many respects there's nothing "populist" about this revival. In reality it's the prestidigitation of the electronic media that is working to cash in on the latest pop culture fad: like the manufacturers of the yo-yo, hula hoop, and Rubik's Cube before them, they are the ones generating the interest, creating the phenomenon to suit themselves and turn a profit along the way. Like most buzz-words, catch phrases, or product names the term "spoken word" is at best a "cool" but confusing misnomer. At worst it's critically barren: a safe, meaningless phrase intended to take the stigma (the craft and actual magic) out of writing poetry, a label that makes the private, adolescent scribblings once thankfully safeguarded in the diaries and journals of young and secretly aspiring writers an exploitable "public domain" for the entertainment industry.

The book you now hold will unveil a world of sacred incantations and magical places; its purpose is to deconstruct the smoke and mirrors of the "spoken word" and without any sleight of hand give you access to the dangerous face of contemporary Canadian poetry as it really is: an innovative, edgy, political, sexual, and textually complex poetic terrain ready to challenge the possibilities of language and life.

It's because of the writers — because of their writing — that this is *The Last Word*. Everyone collected in this book has written and published important, provocative poems over the course of the last few years. They may not be household names — *yet* — but they are what Canadian poetry is about to become. *The Last Word* doesn't, therefore, pretend to simply showcase a collection of "new," "young," "hip" or "great" poets. Instead, its aim is to represent the best of the wide range — in terms of style, thematic concern, political and theoretical intent, and voice — of poetry currently being written in Canada. In *The Last Word* you will find the visual and dub poets beside the lyricists, and confessional or surrealist poets beside the language-based writers. In concrete terms, *The Last Word* is modelled after the "real" world. The one that existed before the "spoken word" — the one that will exist long after its 15 minutes are up.

The historical accident of a small, insular group of people deciding to meet once a month to read poems to each other just as *The New Canadian Poets* was hitting the bookstore shelves is almost inconsequential: there's no important story for the keepers of CanLit history secreted somewhere between the doors of that café and the covers of that book. In fact, there is only one tangible correlation: somehow, for some reason, it was around that time that all across the country the "next generation" of Canadian poets was learning how to write. The last ten years of Canadian poetry cannot be reduced to the rediscovery of the pyrotechnics of performance art; and it cannot be characterized as a group or movement of disaffected youth leading a populist revival. It's been about reading and writing, about investigating and charting and pushing the limits of craft, form, and content. This anthology is a survey and "sample" of what 51 of these explorers — men and women from all across the country — have produced.

One final word: having the opportunity to edit this collection has been a rare and wondrous gift. Within these pages I've gathered words and voices that have, quite simply, shaped my life. Any acknowledgment of their beauty, innovation, or importance, however, belongs — as always — to the writers. Again, for me poetry has always been about reading and learning how to read. That's why proceeds from the sale of *The Last Word* will go to Frontier College in support of the nationwide literacy programmes they charitably and tirelessly administrate. The generosity of these 51 poets goes beyond the "gift" of their writing: every last one of them has graciously donated their work to make this project possible. My greatest hope is that after reading this collection you will be inspired to repay their generosity: *go to the nearest bookstore and buy one of their books.* And if they tell you they don't have the collection in stock, don't give up — remember, *you have the last word* — make them give you the poetry you *want* and *deserve.*

— *michael holmes,*
Toronto, 21/05/95

Carrie Leigh's Hugh Hefner Haiku

— Lynn Crosbie

Hef brings me flowers
tiger lilies, ochre veined
downcast, sleek black cups

small shadows, are the
puckers in his pyjamas
where his skin caves in

tired profligate, I
sigh and pour the oil along
your circular sheets

thinking of all the
times, or women on this bed
glossy old bunnies

I imagine their
breasts, plate of fried eggs, a row
of tonsured monks' heads

his tongue slithers, gaunt
voluptuary, ugly
old man, my eyes close

when I roll his name
Ner. along my tongue, like the
line of cold test tubes

thin bottled semen,
he wants to plant it, deeply
in my flat belly

Hugh junior, and, or
Carietta, a child is
packed in dry blue ice

in silk pyjamas
they have an emperor's crest
it is dark in there

but it's cold as
the green jacuzzi, bubbles
are clouds on its face

I will crush the glass
with the fingers in his back
and pile on my rings

and all the fur coats
and move down the circular
stairs, bloated with gold

the flowers are a
venus-flytrap, with red curls
flames and noxious breath

his betrayal gives
me granite fists, girls scatter
movie stars crumple

as I run away,
from the gaudy prison cell,
of tinsel and skin

I'll sue him and write
and build a home, in the
desert, on the sun

a sequined empress,
a mirage — in loungewear and
harlequin glasses

Saturday Night Fever

— **Lynn Crosbie**
I'm going nowhere
  somebody help me
    somebody help me there

His white suit a peerless lily the wide lapels
an allegorical breastplate. the *Prima Porta Augustus*,
his arm-divine is raised to the glittering ceiling.
    I am the little cupid that clings to
        his thigh — symbolizing Venus, Venus
Goddess of love that I am. when he holds me and we dance,
    my cool silk dress skims my thighs, arouses me and I am
more than a woman,

more than a woman when I defile his neck,
his spotless collar with coral — the pink/orange skeleton:
my lips are jewellery. but as my body pushes closer,
the membrane (the colony) of my desire, he moves, elegantly,
easily, from me

there are two kinds of girls — and nice girls don't —
   push him into the car   Bobby C and Double J
dangerous, circling outside. his gold chains are hot on
         my breastbone —
white bliss when he pushes my skirt higher, higher — *heaven,*
and stops: *just give me a blow job.*

that night I experienced love, not love. wanting
all of him, he looks away, wanting more. the Brooklyn Bridge,

a temple-icon at his throat. I see his dreams are hopeless,
small. and still, I follow him. to the hardware store, and finger
nails screws rakes. I want him to brush my body with Plaster of Paris,
cool enamel paint, until I am pale, bridal, the tender moon.

to show him that there are *sublunary lovers,* that there is
nothing between his fine chalk suits, his blue work smock:

mutability and constancy: there are spheres, turning endlessly
in the skies. where angels sing in *a harmony of ravishing beauty.*

I decide to sleep with him instead. there is a selection of
   condoms in my hand when I reach for him
outside the 2001. the science-fiction of the evening;

he slaps them to the ground, as if I am alien,
clinical, devouring. and walks, incurious of longing,
  space.

Joey is pacing the sidewalk, in perilous platforms, crying
call me Tony, call me — are you going to call me Tony?

I am plotting revenge, a night of abandon, near
oblivion, I do not recognize him, my subjectivity —
doubled

envying his power, despising his weakness

(that) car is idling, when Tony approaches. his face is
  battered, still lovely, his life is changing: this night,
I drink moonshine from a flask and lay down between his
  friends as we drive. strange tongues, teeth assail me,
he asks: *are you happy, are you happy now?* his disgust
  is a tonic

I close my eyes at the whiteness the
glare of their exposed underwear, I imagine
they are vulnerable, that I dictate their
yearning: *how deep is your love,* your love

I thought I wouldn't cry, it felt like something,
something better than

loneliness, anguish: Joey is climbing the golden spires
of the bridge

exultant and desperate. he is showing them, he is showing me
that there are times

when your chest splits and separates and there is your heart.
broken, beating, there are such terrible miracles

his body demolished beneath the water, my screams
exalting him.

I let them lead me away, because they are afraid. but it is this:
the sweet descent of his dauntless body, the
healing black water, a dark coronet

that bears him below and carries him, it carries me to safety.

Paul Teale, Mon Amour

— Lynn Crosbie

*My story is a love story, but only those tortured by love
can understand what I mean.*
— Martha Beck

Before you were apprehended you learned to calculate,
statistical averages
        that two and two would recur at random, I too
matriculate. Blonde on blonde, the malevolent look of love.

I called out to you as they folded you into the armoured car,
my letters secreted to your cell and examined
by censorious guards,

who are heartless and not divine.

You convey your affection with static hands, the demotic of the manacles
the metal links that mediate when I flush each night,
it is like a fever

when your innocent limbs collide with mine, your tender ministrations.
Combing the tangles from my hair, there are scissors placed safely
       behind you,
anaesthetizing me; your endearments enter the fragile tissue

the soft vistas of my wrists and elbows, drawing blood. And you draw tremors
on my spine, with surgical intention, a theatre of lariats and silver duct
       tape,
silver is the crown

that compels my silence. I am on my knees, subject to the choreography
       of zippers,
arcane briefs;

you have entered me, the song of angels in my sleep, such pretty girls.
I say that we are meant for each other, because you are blameless, your sweet
face an act of contrition, and I

petition for your release, and ask you to see. A room of velvet pillows,
       rich red wine,

opera, solitude. Cruel images, hidden under your lies and laces; I
      will be stern, and
forgiving,

men have such obscure desires. Just look at his eyes,
      as untroubled, as clear as the sea that rages
in me; I will confess then, in the shadows of our secret evenings,
      you are not a stranger.
If you are kind to me, there is nothing else.

Their pristine bodies, helpless beneath saws and bindings that
      are not apocryphal,
the shock of flowers on their graves. Confectionery terror,
      my delight, since you have spared
me, I am precious — heaven's delicacy,

your own duplicate, a killer without conscience, with an appetite
      that even you, and your vicious
longings, can not requite.

the mortician's waltz

— damian lopes

awhereness

— damian lopes

colonized & colonizer
passports from a colonizer & a colony   a citizen of both
passing ports   never stopping   like passing go
i feel no split

my mother too is colonized & colonizer
scottish mother & english father
born in india (like her mother) six years before independence
more colonized than colonizer from childhood

my father's parents went to tanganyika territory as colonizers
from a differently colonized part of india
conceived under the british protectorate
emigrating before independence

born in scotland & taken away soon after
don't speak to me of dispossession   unhousement
i experienced that countless times before i was born
then i was born & taken away again
i've no memory of scotland
going back was new
the empress of canada
temporary home in water
i don't remember   then an apartment
that means nothing though it's part of me somewhere
a suburban house   converted duplex

one house with two master bedrooms & two kitchens
a/way station for my father's brothers & their families
as they left to come to canada
from birthplaces in east africa
new homes in scotland with step-children
my father's parents left home again after forty years

when my mother left   i was left
one ex-duplex & one two bedroom basement apartment
puzzled about what a home apart meant
owning & renting   landlord & tenant   my pair rents
assuming & subsuming   a different apartment & meanings shift
two houses   two homes   new variations   a wooden house
back to the second which had changed back to the first now a house
i made mine until summer & then left

                              to begin a new language

The Men of My Dreams

— Margaret Webb

I have to stop blowing
men
up
in my dreams

it's hard
to make
love
to the fragments

Night Time

— Margaret Webb

I have the world
the stars, the sun and the moon
in the smiling face
of my wrist watch

and last night I had
my brother's head
between my legs

points of stars swelling
until

our mother came
to the foot of the bed
watching

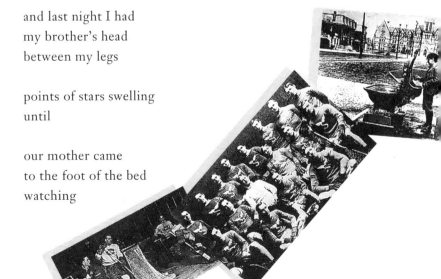

we are 14 and 15 and don't know anything
except

we'd have fucked each other
dead

until the tiny moon
on my watch
went down
and the sun came up

Walking With My Husband One Night...

— **Margaret Webb**

then we were walking home and he jumped out of
the bushes and tried to drag me off

you hung on to one arm while he pulled on the other

then we were at the bus stop and he leapt out of
the shelter and tried to rape me

you hung on to one arm while he pulled on the other

then we were turning down our street and he tried to
grab my purse

you said, let it go, it's not worth risking your life over

my one arm being free, I swung and knocked him out

Phatic Weather

— Jeff Derksen

I just want
the connection to be
inked in or intruded
on. So I can enter

an individual history
of my group.

The truck driving
beside the bus
appears not to move, mimicking
a model of one culture
viewing another.

Here the light
to heavy industry
doesn't mar the river
as much as it now
makes it.

New. Compensation's body
is a green image, arms
filled with lumber. But production's
miracle is its occurrence, oiling
a century. Our role
is the crisis. Sliding
so I can clarify
a centralized management

in this continuous present
of product, "excess," resource.

A company's head office
puts down roots: "Caring Hands
Extended Out to Our Multicultural
Community." The question

of "also" is contextual.

Excursive 4

— Jeff Derksen

Bread stacked like wood. Tourism as a method of state control
for a specific region. After he's had a few glasses he keeps
repeating the toast "The best wine in the world, better than
German wine." In small towns, dogs live on top of the flat-
roofed houses, running around the peripheries, looking down,
barking, straining. Later, I'm told that "Fuera Godos" refers to
Spaniards from the peninsula who have come to the islands to
set up businesses. With the unusually high tide, men are fishing
at midnight in the tiny manmade lagoon that is the Germans'
sunning area during the day. The bartender was in the
Merchant Marines and wants to talk about how cold Canada is.
Sunset drive from Bajamar to La Laguna with Tony Bennett or
someone on the radio with an inspirational song (here the buses
are called *guaguas*, and this is the longest sentence I have writ-
ten on one). As I wrote that sentence, we passed into another
microclimate, moving from the town that grows grapes for the
wine into the town that supplies the island with carrots.

Remembering the past tense has added time to my conversations. Usually a rented "Panda" or "Seat Ibeza" with a man driving and a woman looking at an unfolded map. Imperialism at the level of the syllable makes "un cafe" an insistent "*ein* cafe." Out of necessity, I've added all words concerning the *tracto orinario* (urinary tract) to my vocabulary. Our Canadian sense of scale carries over to maps. He means to insult me, calling me a "maricon" (homosexual), which I confuse with *marisco* (shellfish). We want to know about food, wines, and where it's cheap, that is, we reproduce our role earnestly. A tapas of boiled octopus. During Carnaval, with the jammed streets, men can piss anywhere — a favourite spot is on the side of a large bank, but not the church as much. I don't speak Spanish Do you speak English How are you I am well Not too good. It seems that because the red flags are signs for the Spanish words "*mar peligroso,*" the German-speaking tourists don't think it applies to them. The dilapidated beauty (or only because it is dilapidated) of the Hotel Neptuno. The pleasure of the. On Sundays, because of the *autopista* that bisects the island, families drive out to restaurants for the afternoon meal: this particular Sunday driver is called a "Domingera." Bar Nuevo Obrero, Bar Estoy Aqui, Bar Quatro Caminos, Bar La Oficina, Bar Sandalio, Bar Los Huevos Duros, Bar El Nervioso, Bar Restaurant Snack Bar, Bar Stop. The dog's ability to simultaneously ignore and follow you across town. Standing in the small local restaurant, reading a photocopied page taped to the wall (which caught my attention because of its "Workers' Party" logo), the first sentence is "As usual the Canary government has put tourism ahead of the people of Bajamar and Punta Hidalgo . . ." — of course they're watching me read it. Wood stacked like bread. I experience simple feelings in Spanish.

from Ten or so

— C.M. Donald

When I was eleven, precocious brat,
I discovered the local theatre (weekly rep.)
let schoolkids in cheap.

                Parents shrugged — I went
weekly. Saw *Salad Days* — very
cheering. Saw *King Lear* — complete
        incomprehension. Saw
Ibsen's *Ghosts* — loved that, something
way over my head about a family, something
very wrong with the family, which I
couldn't articulate — loved that.

        Oh and Romberg's musical *New Moon* where the
villain had a great scar all down his cheek
and fell in love with the leading
lady but of course he wasn't
allowed to have her — loved that;
wanted a scar all down my cheek
to mark me too.

                •

And then there was the time
you gave my dolls' house away.
Simple. I came home,
looked over the garden wall;
the girl next door was playing with it.

Later in therapy, the dolls' house

again, worn a little
thin.

      Tell you what, mother.
You were right — I didn't mind
about the toy.
          Took me a long time, though,
to identify the feeling: cold shock
as mother's love appeared
on the other side of the fence.

Beuys

— Sky Gilbert
I had my choice between Beuys
and boys
I don't know
Some choose Beuys
Peter did
As for me, though I find Beuys nice
I still choose boys.
After all when Beuys walks into the sea
you know it's because of Kierkegaard or Steiner
But boys
they're a different matter
They walk into the sea because the night calls them
because they're lonely.

or because the sea is wet
And they don't ... come back
I repeat, don't
So if I had my choice
I'd take boys
their thighs are bigger
and they don't come back
(sorry, Joseph).

Confession number one

— **Sky Gilbert**

Alright, one more
And this is an early movie
One of the earliest The Postman Rings Twice
In Postman Lana is almost quadruply outclassed by the terse,
dark script, by the taut direction and by Cecil Kellaway and
John Garfield both consummate actors with real talent
But Lana has something that outclasses everything and everyone
The camera loves her in a way that reminds us of what love is all
about for just as our eye constantly turns to the loved one to
devour to observe every detail every batting of an eye of flinch
of muscle the camera cannot get enough of her and she knows it
When she says "I've never been homely but ever since I was
fourteen I've never met a man who didn't give me an argument
about it"
We understand and we understand that love is an argument and
that beauty always wins
Evil again, she pouts and plans but most of all she offers her lips
her eyes her hips and those outfits of classic white (a different

one in every scene) there is so much to savour — there's Lana burst-
ing out of the diner in the dead of night in her swimming garb, hair
perfectly coiffed and swinging her bathing cap with daring insouciance.
What is more daring even than sex with John Garfield under the
moonlight is going swimming with that hairdo
Will it get mussed?
But no, the blindness and faith of moviegoers in the '40s was such
that Lana could endure sickness death and even midnight skinny dip-
ping without damaging that hair
And in the silence of his bedroom
For at the crucial moment she slips into John Garfield's bedroom and
John Garfield registers for us the ecstasy the surprise the utter
delightful confusion of such beauty suddenly appearing in one's bedroom
And Lana quivering there her shoulders hunched intensely as we
imagine the fall of her breasts the nipples delicately grazing the
starched white cotton fabric
"A woman needs love."
Yes Lana, yes like John Garfield we forgive your ambition, we forgive
your lies your plotting your planning we even forgive your fake movie
ironing
because we want to kiss you the way we want to kiss that person we
shouldn't, you know the one that every instinct tells us will lead to
sleepless nights and bad phone calls and a general difficulty in dealing
with anything that's supposed to be important
We want to kiss you the way John Garfield does
And we know that he's whispering to himself
"I must ... I must ... even if it means my own ... someone else's
death ... I must kiss her ... I must ..."
He grabs her shoulders her muscles tense, the lips pout and they
plunge into the darkness, the oblivion, the ecstasy which is their lust

Drivin' and Cryin'
— Robyn Cakebread

stop the car, she cried and the wind let her hair fall, lingering in the ends. she loves this song and turns it up as the car rolls across the gravel, to a halt. a hot day, heavy. good for leaving. she remembered the name of the guy she had slept with who had only one leg. the music is slow, a ballad with heart-wrenching lyrics, streaming from an agonized young man in too-tight pants. it was the pants that reminded her. her boyfriend had been upstairs the whole time, and they had slipped into the basement to do it quickly. they had danced all night, except when she vomits across an unoccupied shoe. he told her about how he loved to ride his bicycle. it hadn't seemed they were gone long, but everyone had left the party by the time he had replaced his prosthetic. the plastic felt suave and complicated, strong and she liked that. it had squeaked loudly and threatened to dampen the mood. he had wondered, would she mind if he removed it. she drinks some pineapple juice, sticky and sweet on her lips. a drop falls into her lap, swelling round on the leg of her jeans. she really thought they were in love, you know. the next day it was all like a dream until the phone rang and the screaming voice on the other end sparked a fear in her that made it real again. her hands tremble a little, fumbling in her shiny purse for a cigarette. she laughs. the car heads out into the traffic, peeling past a bright yellow Dodge. sun streams down on her nose, sitting under dark glasses, turning it a soft shade of pink. behind the glasses, she dabs small veins of black, mingling with purple, red, brown. stunned by the slow rush of emotion, she runs a hand through her hair, pulling it into a tight curl on

top of her head, tucking the frizzy blonde ends under. outside the sky shines bright grapefruit red. trees, dizzy from the lack of shade, whip by in flashes of green and brown. the road has no end, just white lines that curve and dip. true, she declares, that it was wrong. a good thing to be leaving there, because what else could she do. she felt cold, she said and the sun is much nicer. a smile. cold when he touched her. all those stupid costumes and weird toys were not her thing. but she loved him, her boyfriend, and could not really say why, except that she felt like a child again when they were together. when they laughed. he was pretty, like a doll, ruby cheeks, black hair, clear-pale skin. one Valentine's day they had wine, very romantic. she wore red lingerie, red nail polish, lipstick, and ate cinnamon hearts to freshen her breath. he would like this, her looking sexy. right when they were going to express their love, he turned her over, he didn't want to see her face. the next day she rubbed hard with cotton and polish remover but the red was in deep under her cuticle. now she knows that red polish is tacky. she prefers opalescent shades. a man plucks the strings of his guitar, slow and melodic, he sings poetry. this is how she feels, she says, when she is floating. she pulls her sweater around her shoulders as the sky light falls away. before her, red flashes reflect across the surface of her glasses.

now i'm burned

— Robyn Cakebread

Cigarette smoke drifts, heavily, up from the hand that should be reaching out to my kid, and other people I can think of. Are they here? Thinking is so difficult these days, so, I sit here looking around my home. What used to be my safe place, I've

moved though, further inside.

I can see everything around me, one-dimensional:

blue carpet
blue couch
blue chairs
blue memories that make me blue.

I feel the difficulty roaring around somewhere, blocked by my daughter's laughter, my husband grunting, as I sleep. He grunts while I sleep. It took some time but then I felt it there, like a dream I couldn't shake off, but of course it was real and he is much heavier in

lifetime than dreamtime.

Didn't want him, not then or before which is why he does it now, thinking I'm too asleep to notice. I am deadlike. He likes this. I remember ghosts while I am dead, lying on me and to me

a grunt a ghost a grunt a ghost.

High up on a fence I climb, higher, down, so small, I feel I must be bloating. Floating over the fence and out, into another back-yard. A new world full of surprises, like:

rockgarden
short shrubs
a path of flagstone.

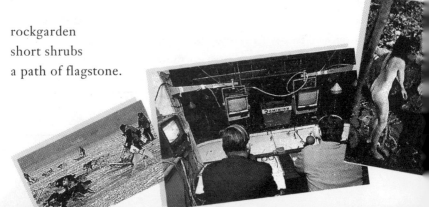

I am ten and I follow the flagstone out onto a street. Now I am far far away from home. will they notice I am gone, or, in how long?

Flick. The flickering of the television, I flickmybic, and I'm so tired again. What I want is some happiness, inside. Happiness makes me lighter, I think the ads say it's

theotherwayaround.

There is a picture of a woman in a white dress smiling at a man who is smiling at her. I think I can see something, there, that I didn't used to see, or maybe I can't see it now, what was there. Baby pictures, too many to count.

Crying now, I've woken someone. I hear wailing and feel my body heaving, but no one is home. I have been left alone, finally. Isn't that what I wanted, to be left alone? In numb seclusion, so I left that twelve-year-old place and moved into another age. Away from that, my body is
larger
heavier
scarcely enough.

Once I sizzled, now I'm burned.

My arm reaches down. It hits the floor quickly, sooner than I expected. It is a burden to lift it again, so I lie down with it. Gravity is so helpful. I lie down in my home. I try so hard to keep things

clean
vacuumed
washed
ready.

But I can see where I have failed, from here. From here you can
see the mess I've made. Too many toys, an old sock, a missing
button, a shoe, a pill bottle. It's

empty.

The Inside Dog

— Mac McArthur

i.
She was a gull I found in morning.
Lake, seaway and river from her sense of salt.
I scooped the feathers and opened skin
(picked of what was missing)
and added her to trimmings to burn
when weather permits me to make smoke.
Outside this place is violent.

ii.
A window to the past is not instant recovery.
I am aware of the smells of a dead father's straps
when his ankles come back to me as pets. For me to pat.

To curl up umbilical (head to toe)
inside what was his cold and is now grounded.
Not dangerous, not a threat.

I also live with animals.
We check the evening's breathings,
each having had masters and servants die on us unexpectedly.

And what we divine is the events we form
(not always by pretence or the mind):
those within the finer particles of mist,
at odd angles and often salient.

iii.
The first tree by the door nears a hundred. Is not final.
Double old enough to grow moss and hold more than one species.
This year it pits a nest of wasps against a nest of birds.
      I avoid the conflict.

And winter is one more closed edge
with the deer anxious for my salt lick and lower branches.
Terrified of my foot's pause on ice over snow.
The breads I scatter catch a scent, chase it, lose it
and lie down victims, frozen cubes inedible and lost.
The listing and the list of stones goes on. Goes on.

What is this place after all but another part of where I live!
The place outside this house is violent.
There is no longer violence within.

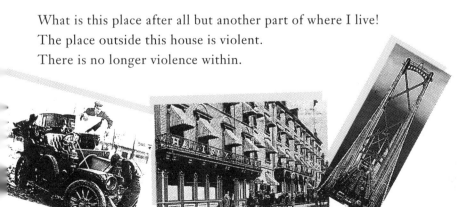

iv.

Like me, the inside dog stands her wet fur to the fog.
First the hairs and then her head come back to me
when we wander home, with a side-growl
if her mood is challenged. And she is moody.
The nipples are white not wet,
        not used after births and sudden deaths.

Witness,
I watched double incidents (natural but for intervals)
of what we acknowledge on floors but standing won't discuss.
She has an older step and it's only been three days.

We (the dog and I) notice each other.
Nothing more than that at times.

My First S+M Experience
— Sonja Mills

    Laura-Lee McFarland and I were 10 years old in grade four. Best friends; we spent every day together, and I would sleep over at her house every weekend. Her house was better than my house, because she didn't have brothers or sisters and she had her own TV in her bedroom in the basement, two whole floors away from her parents, so they couldn't hear us. We would drink whole big bottles of ginger ale, eat potato chips and watch the baby blue movies that came on late at night. We watched women sucking on guys' dinks and tried to see how it would feel

by sucking on each other's fingers. I could almost get her whole hand in my mouth, but not quite.

One of our favourite games was to sneak into the garage when her parents were sleeping, beat the fuck out of each other with her dad's tools — then crawl back into her bed and push each other's bruises all night.

One hot summer night in the garage, we had nothing but our pyjama bottoms on: two smooth, skinny, flat-chested girls. Laura-Lee hit my arm with something we hadn't tried before — a flat wooden carpenter's ruler. The pain was different than when she hit me with hammers or wrenches. It hurt more I think — but it was sweeter. She liked it too. Liked the way it sounded and the way my skin welted a bit where she hit it.

She asked if I wanted to play cowboys and indians. I liked that game a lot. She tied my hands together with rope as usual, threw it up over one of the rafters and while I stood on my toes and reached up as high as I could; she pulled the rope tight and tied it to the garage door, so I was sort of half-hanging, half-standing on my toes. I can't remember why we called that game cowboys and indians.

She hit me again with the ruler across my arms and shoulders and back. Hard. Each smack harder and sweeter until I flinched and yelled a bit without knowing it. She shushed me — "don't wake up my parents."

Then, without warning — that little girl pulled my pyjama bottoms down around my ankles and started hitting my bum and the backs of my legs and I got that funny weird feeling in my little, hairless cunt that I sometimes got when I slept at her house. I didn't know what to do when I got that feeling in my cunt. Sometimes I still don't.

When she was finished she wanted us to go in and get some pop — but I told her to go ahead and just bring some out. She was gone for a long time it seemed, and I just hung there — feeling the time pass, feeling every inch of my stinging flesh — and liking it, and not liking it, and then liking it again. And something else. Something I hadn't felt before. Left alone, hanging, stinging, exposed, pants down around my ankles and not a thing I could do about it... I felt something I knew I was going to want to feel again — I was humiliated.

And I don't know, but maybe if I hadn't played those games in the fourth grade with Laura-Lee McFarland, maybe I wouldn't understand why pain and why humiliation — can be so provocative.

A Winter Scene

— Sonja Mills

The girl and I come home from a long night of grinding our cunts together on a dance floor (well, we have to go out and be sociable sometimes). We've had the first major snowfall of the winter — four inches of good, wet packing snow. We romp and play in it like puppies walking down the street from the subway and when we get to the house, decide to build a snow-dyke on the front lawn.

We name her Lou: a truck-driving snow-bitch with big tits

and a moustache. And as the girl is finishing up — leaned over, attaching a rolled-up ring of foil from her cigarette package through our snow-mama's left nipple — I pelt her ass with a snowball. Her reaction is more severe than I expected. She tackles me and rolls with me through the wet muck, pulling at my clothes, grabbing my tits and telling me she wants to fuck me right here in front of all the neighbours.

I laugh and put my hands on the sides of her head. I want to pull her face close to mine so I can kiss her; but with an evil smirk she shovels a handful of snow down my pants. It's so cold I squeal and piss myself a little...

She notices.

Car

— Tony Burgess
Not ready to be left behind
I built a car.
I pulled its arms in, and
filled it with spores.

I will cruise in my car,
not like a space man. No.
I'll find a lucky clover leaf
and trace it with my summer tires.

But I am a space man, after all.
A bumper car lined with ice,
Knees pulled up to its chest
With chopped off hands I built it.

Poem
— Tony Burgess

I am a magnet drawing
            nearer
curdled voice
seeps backwards
  call
run a jackal
      wet
honesty

targets spinning
      free
bled
loose

spitting roses
thousand pretty

pinned there
talking
making eyes
whipping posts
  round sounds hollow halos

  just as it was getting light
the night   dead in breezes
I watched
my arms from me
Like wings unwarmed

Hope

— Tony Burgess

I hope you are stupid
I hope I am smart
I hope that you lose track of me,
I've hidden things.

Café au Lait

— Nicole Markotić

four women drinking café au lait. in a bowl. I always insist on a
    bowl. four women slurping up caffeine. breakfast begins
    with coffee, and this the only

Monique teaches History in Prince Rupert. same school as her
    husband. who has a 15-year-old lover and new baby. she
    doesn't tell me this, you do. two and two. women

I learned to drink from a bowl the summer I spent in Québec

in the café women slurp caffeine. I say caffeine gives me
    migraines. a woman with red hair, black jacket, red belt,
    black leather boots, red tassels passes by the café window
    three times. I watch the boy who stands around the corner

holding flowers wilting in the sun. doesn't he know enough to
    wait for her in the shade? you say, laughing at the poor
    boy, ripped jeans, long uncombed hair, pimples. and a
    bouquet of elegance, tradition, waste. we women laugh

the laugh the voice the sign. the recognition

when I spent five days crying, non-stop, you didn't expect. but:
    I'm not even sad anymore, just pissed off, where the hell is
    all this damn liquid coming from. you let me cry five days.
    no stopping. without once

he curves his back against a telephone booth and resists the
        compulsion to make the phone call. the one where she gets
        to say:

stop. now. when I *do* stop, completely, you don't tell me how I
        shouldn't laugh so much. I laugh

the obvious hazy smile the boy insists on carrying. the sun
        beating up the roses. I laugh hardest. finish my café au
        lait first. at this moment, before we walk back to your car,
        I understand that the smile means she isn't coming, her
        day too crammed with details. and that smile, *my* smile,
        means he knows she won't. not for him, not even for roses

the crying was only me. the noise and the tears and the ranting
        against. you, late at night, open, listening to the gulp of
        tears, to the lack of smile. you: offered possibility. Prince
        George and Churchill, Manitoba. Alaska and New Zealand

four women. two plus two. the one who teaches drives off with
        her friend from Colorado. we fortify ourselves with coffee,
        with the sweet slurp of elegance. there was something
        closed about [he] I say to you. after
what I understand: that smile means total joy

that smile believes what it has to believe: that she must be coming
        because how could she not? I still think: how could she
        not?

Connect the Dots:

— Nicole Markotić

I am not who I say I am. buses don't run backwards, and god's
not a man, he's somebody else

tell me who you are tell me who you are tell me who you are tell
me who you   wait   wait

> the gold   the chipped pot   the arrow ending   the rainbow
> the nothing   the much ado about   the undoing
> the woman's face in   your moon face   the bow
> the no more time fors   the not now
> my   name

between my apartment and my job stretch two playground zones:
30 k/per hour: 30 k. I crawl back home in the afternoons

I have two nieces, both [he]'s. I have a sister, 7 1/2 months
pregnant. she won't let the doctors induce her labour. I own a
see-through telephone, the plastic numbers light up when I dial

except: in the morning, driving away from the me, I speed all the
way

gold rush
— Mark Sinnett

You died,

and in sorting things we found maps
in lace-lined drawers beside your bed.
They were stained with tea or else,
we decided, were old as the hills.

Somewhat more remote
was the possibility you baked
the paper to this brittle state,
& honest to that notion

we inspected cookie trays
like Columbo (a quick search
we emerged from moody).
The path shown was known to us;

it ran around back of barns
that as kids we hid in,
learning to make rhymes.
And it led — past thick stream, over-

hanging willow — to graves
beyond the churchyard's wall,
three mounds little more
risen than camber, and too short,

we thought, for other than dogs.
We came to dig, though, and did —
past dark, the stone wall swung
around us like cloak, air

become by night wet, heavier
than the bones we threw white
into the sky, and which — in so arcing —
were animate and a treasure to us.

The Wading Pool

— Mark Sinnett

The wading pool, its skin-thick water set
deep into concrete basin, going green
with algae, brings me here. To a park cut
out of old cemetery, graves now swung
or swum over oblivious. I kick
at the ground, though, dislodge from clay thin-boned
shin, a doctor's back tooth, and keep an eye
on the lifeguard who thinks writing a trick,
these words a twisted rope just now wound
to lure her away. In the shade I try
to arrange my body to reflect hers,
its look as unconscious of form as those
children she protects, the splashing monsters
her moves come from: the jutted hip, few clothes.

This Claimer

— Ahdri Zhina Mandiela

not
a commentary.
presumed socially significant/except
a channel/my
creative/pipe to
let out/blocked hopes.

these words are/for/ever/
more/just fossilled:
language

& this: one
of many/million
dark tales

Dark diaspora

— Ahdri Zhina Mandiela

check
the blues dance affair
passing
in brown paper
bottles, tarnished by a 100
militant skank: rub-a-dub
rumbling revellers
in red hot civilian fatigue
chanting arms
in the dark diaspora

welcome broke bookmakers
as they close shop/tune in
to the midnite parade: hear
airwaved pirated blues/no
commerce news of flatfoot marketeers
jingling pound weight/
sensi: legal trade
in the dark diaspora

listen to lyrical lectures/
hurry-come-bring
linguistic reflections: reality/
chucksing style

in tight-roped poster panache
in the dark diaspora

finger the free-formed
cultural remnants, etched
on immaculate sheets of black
while/plain-painted stages
stand accused/piping
solo versions
of memories bubbling resistance
in the dark diaspora

follow the northwest detour: south
parade down soca-
lined streets
in search of carnival sceptres:
madwomen & hustlers
born of infected morning rain
echoing the pain
of pans
beating our distant
suns/and
daughters thirst forever
drinking 30 years
of immigrant legacy
in the dark diaspora

in the dark diaspora
here cameras work on gear/shift
without reverse/into
tomorrow's resolution
moving rhythms
of yesteryear's birthing

to expose the martyred skulls
of forgotten victory

& rub-a-dub tracks
replay the rumbling of revellers
chanting arms
viva! *mandela*/chanting arms
garvey forever/chanting arms
say it/say it/say it
say it loud/i'm black
& i'm proud/say it loud
black black black
black/gay gay gay/hey
say it loud/come what may
we're here to stay/
rally round/*jah! rastafari*
a luta continua...
sanctions now/sanctions now/
by any means necessary/we shall overcome/
our will be done today/
after 50 eons of black tracks/
better mus come!

chanting arms
chanting arms
chanting arms
chanting

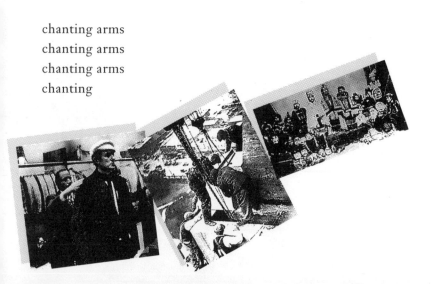

Label

— W. Mark Sutherland

No: _____   Title:_____   Poet:_____

Date:_____   Time: _____

Equipment Used:	Voice	_____	Computer	_____
	Pencil	_____	Video	_____
	Pen	_____	Film	_____
	Typewriter	_____	Tape Recorder	_____

Form:	Prose	_____	Verse	_____
	Dithyramb	_____	Concrete	_____
	Epic	_____	Sonnet	_____
	L=a=n=g=u=a=g=e	_____	Sound	_____

Use of:	Analogy	_____	Allegory	_____
	Allusion	_____	Euphemism	_____
	Hyperbole	_____	Metaphor	_____
	Metonymy	_____	Synecdoche	_____

Location:_____

Atmospheric Conditions: _____

Historical Conditions: _____

Sociological Conditions: _____

Political Conditions: _____

Economic Conditions: _____

Additional Observations: _____

_____

_____

_____

A Moment Later

— W. Mark Sutherland

...splashes its contents
over a white table cloth

...disturbing. Although made
of synthetic material clotted
with glue

...raw humour leaves a ring
on the rough floor

...images drained. Frozen in
life-like poses for a benevolent
camera

...distance from the skin
of an electrical chord

...conflicts and unforgiving
context freed from gravity

...re-enter the room and avoid
tripping on the centre
of calm

...every difference exposed

...more and more energy
taken up

...chronicles of experience

...in doubt

Encoding Verlaine's Chanson D'Automne

— W. Mark Sutherland

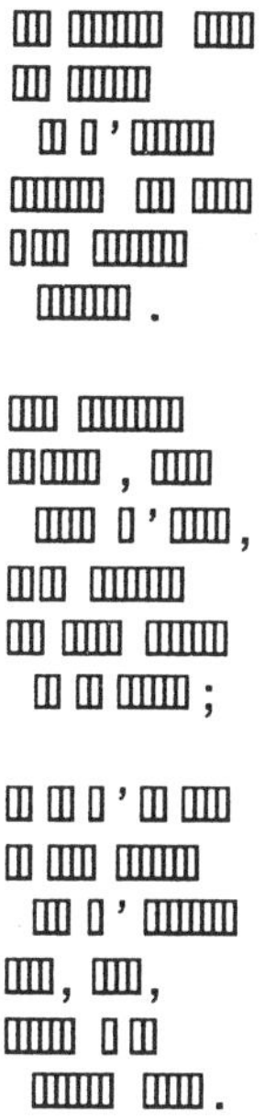

██ ██████ ████
██ ██████
  ██ █'█████
██████ ██ ████
███ ██████
  █████ .

███ ███████
█████ , ███
  ████ █'████,
███ ██████
██ ████ ██████
  ██ ██ █████ ;

██ ██ █'██ ████
██ ███ █████
  ██ █'██████
███, ███,
█████ █ ██
  █████ ████.

Dear M:

— Nancy Shaw

Since our extraordinary conversation, I have thought of little else — of your studied coldness and beautiful little cigarette. I must admit to you that when the curtain rose on that dimly lit bar I listened without interest — in an atmosphere drenched with novelty and surprise. There was no evidence that this letter was actually sent to anyone. On the contrary, the deviant scenes scarcely seemed to have been mentioned. When the dishevelled man rushed in, he stood half-fashioned and politely yet fiendishly recommended a long, eloquent, moving expression of transfigured love. He never quite regained our affection. We were left at liberty to study, criticize and admire his anticipation of a happy future.

Today I got my first compliment as a pixie. Though this does not belong in any story, we were intrigued by such a proposition. I then became associated with my series of passions for other people's lives, most of whom, by the way, I had not met. Among terms so loose, luck held over temperance, liberty and redemption. All the while the writer knew a little Latin and maintained his remarkable talent for affliction. The artist failed to take an interest in the narrator's love of telescopes. As it was her first night out as a brunette, the narrator disguised herself as a swindler, spicing her intentions with little tropes and clever puns.

The writer's clues may throw everything into confusion but he is more than a fatalist. He seeks out trios and contraptions, loafers and imposters. There is a proposition that he will leave, but only with the narrator. The artist famed for his prowess and untamed labour wanders through this over-elaborate mockery.

L.

The Illusion Did Not Last
— **Nancy Shaw**

It began harmlessly with a question:
Who was counter-nature?

After this highly discursive introduction
another small anecdote:
at intervals of an hour
each believed herself
the true heroine.

Supposing she fell into a frenzy
somewhere between
the wish and its fulfillment.

Rumours, and rumours of rumours.
Volumes of heresy.

No longer young
as he once was
the arsonist.

Episodic testimony.

The man on whom the heavy burden
had fallen had no feeling for sights
signalling peril everywhere
in a hectic show of civility.
I thought this was typical

Later, several burning barrels of cordiality.

At least they do not notice
it in themselves
the reading of
a good life
the heroic man
bravely lashing.

Dim sheath;
that I suddenly felt this.

The Pipe Organ
— Matthew Remski

The pipe organ, like language, is an experiment in material
and technological hybridization. This is but one probable narra-
tive:

An organ in a Romanesque cathedral adjoining a monastery on
the rim of the Black Forest is installed, following the return of
the abbot from a visit to the convent in Rupertsberg in 1174,
where he has heard a performance of the *Sequentiae liber divino-*

rum operum given by the composer, the Abbess Hildegard von Bingen, accompanied by a small consort of novices. He contracts the builder of the psaltérion used in the recital, and by April of 1178, a small, single-manual, three-ranked instrument, suitable for simple accompaniments of plainsong, is operational in the choir loft of the cathedral. In August of 1282 it is almost destroyed in a fire. Its scorched casing is replaced by Christmas of that year and painted in time for Easter. In January of 1356, while installing four more ranks in the instrument, the organ builder falls through the top of the casing, and is fatally impaled on the brass trumpets. This prompts the abbot to declare the embellishing project a sin of pride and excess, reparable only by protracted penitential silence. No one plays the new ranks until 1364, except for a few adventurous novices interested in tempting fate with late-night forays into the cathedral. In 1412, a monk whose duties include manually pumping the ten-foot bellows while the organ is played goes mad from exposure to the cadmium used to illuminate manuscripts and slashes the leather bellows to shreds with his stylus. The following week a cow is slaughtered for Shrove Tuesday, and the hide is used to repair the bellows. In June of 1497, the bottom eight pipes of the *Bassflöte* rank, measuring up to 32 feet in length, rot from moisture seeping through the tarred roof. Using lumber from the surrounding forest, replacement pipes are carved, tuned and installed by February of 1498. In 1518, an evangelizing acolyte of Martin Luther is chased to the next village by monks who steal his German-language Bible and his book of Lutheran hymns, some of which are sung at mass the following week. In 1549, the abbot decides that the use of the instrument will no longer be limited to the accompaniment of psalmody. In

September of that year he sends the most promising novice to Paris to study music and performance with Clément Janequin. In 1552, the novice returns and requests that the instrument be updated with a second manual that would have a complement of solo reed stops. These modifications are completed on midwinter solstice, 1554. In 1602, the price of ivory falls in eastern Europe, and the monastery elects to refurbish the modest (and now quite worn) wooden keyboards with ivory coverlets. They purchase too much ivory for the keys alone, and use the remainder to craft icons of the Madonna, to adorn the façade of the tabernacle, or to decorate various instruments used for self-immolation. Over a period of eight months in 1611, the tracking system is entirely rebuilt to incorporate a more sophisticated system of balances. In the interim, all worship is *a cappella*. In 1682, the monastery commissions the organ builders to install a *Brustwerk* manual for greater flexibility in accompaniment. In November of 1704, the pipes of the *Lieblichnasat* are severely damaged by the thrashing of a thirteen-year-old peasant girl as she is raped inside the instrument by the assistant organist. The pipes are moulded and refitted one by one using a lead alloy from Switzerland, and the rank is working by May, at which time the rape victim, now in her third trimester, is executed by the Inquisition for consorting with demons. She is tied to a 16-foot *Bassflöte* carved out of evergreen with cedar fittings, that has warped irreparably in the humidity of the spring. She confesses when the steam from the fire of purification below her creates a faint and unstable tone in the pipe. In July of 1796, the façade pipes are repainted and varnished. In March of 1822, a third manual, the *Rückpositiv*, is added, substantially changing the configuration of the console and the weight of the action.

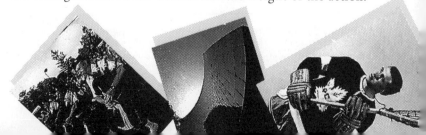

The new division of pipes is installed behind the chair, creating an entirely new acoustic environment for the organist. In September of 1867, the manual blower system is replaced by an electrically-powered fan, and subsequently the abbot can afford to send one of his charges to help in the building and administration of the new chapter in Kitchener, Ontario. The monk is sent with a case of organ-building tools, and whatever superfluous parts (tracker fittings, stop bars) the monastery can spare. A new electric lamp is installed in the music stand in time for the Christmas vigil of 1908, greatly reducing eyestrain, but provoking numerous complaints from liturgical purists. In 1916, the monastery is asked to donate the lumber it had been curing for organ parts to the Fokker warplane construction plant on the Rhine. The abbot signs the release papers and blesses the wood as it leaves in a flatbed wagon. In 1921, a stray burst from a Roman candle lit to celebrate the Feast of Fools (in which novices and younger monks are given authority over their superiors for the day) flies through the rose window over the choir loft, and lands among three Psalters beside the console, left open to the funeral liturgy performed the previous day for a deceased brother. The fire rages all night, destroying the tracking system and 40% of the pipes. By 1923 the pipes have been rebuilt, reinstalled, and reconnected to a new electro-pneumatic activation console with twelve pistons (coded keys allowing instant access to prefigured registrations). In 1940, a German-Jewish family is hidden from the Nazis inside the instrument. The four-year-old son is more frightened by the loudness of the music during Mass than by the shelling of the nearby village. In 1954, two novices are severely punished for carving their names, accompanied by homoerotic avowals of love, onto the inside of

the main encasement. The names are never removed. In 1968, the ivory keys, now yellowed and cracked, are replaced by plastic facsimiles. In 1971, a set of chimes are installed for use in a recital given by John Cage. In 1979, the monastery rents the cathedral for a performance of *Jesus Christ Superstar*, and the top of the casing of the choir division is cracked when it is used as a dancing platform. Aware of the necessity for fiscal restraint, the abbot orders the casing to be patched with plywood left over from the state-sponsored construction of a drug rehabilitation centre, built on land sold off by the monastery to balance debts.

This is the diachrony of the instrument, the etymology of organic systems of signification. Synchrony happens when the entire instrument is heard by someone well-acqainted with this narrative, someone who listens for the real-time difference that is produced by the juxtaposition of historical anomalies. Pipes from the 14th century beside pipes from the 18th century. Through keys, the finger directly touches the ruinous matter of an echoing history. Rape and death in the divisions.

from Low Fancy

— Catriona Strang

Avert sighs, ignore decorum:
> our stops redeem us
whose florid queen's a kiss.
> We tail libation's cult
though time proffers its necessary insult —
> our token penance.

•

Imagine my SURPRISE at finding my own intervention glossed over in a marginal note, a conjectural emendation of three distinct hands and an ungrammatical linger spiked with flickering brawl, as striking as a rotten tapestry's green parrot or the blackening tooth of a mouth whose tongue knows no frontiers. But this MYSTERY's only one of the earliest corrosives in a popular confusion bitten by patterns of repetition, and a gathering intensity that SUCCUMBS to the easy charms of the remote. When was my mood ever untranslatable?

•

Leg it lightly;
memory's an inquest
whose tonic cumbles ethics:
addled, ambulant, and glorious
a becoming bonus.

I'd dispone *any* minimum
and cite supine eras
to prime my dear hocks
so, script, console us: "kiss, sit."
Dignity's done.

•

Christ's dice, it's true.
My dick can rarely, rarely care;
it's as caring as a nun's habit.
Ubiquitous.

It rants an unveiled script
whose visceral ply inveigles
use: "do more, come more" — I'll roam
and bulge a fulminant leave.

Imitating Art

— Murdoch Burnett

Violins are playing now and
well they should. In the movies,
where life imitates art, when the
lover reaches for the lover's hand
what do we hear? Violins are playing
now and well they should. My life
is imitating art, like movies
and I'm reaching for the
hand of a lover.

Violins are playing now
and beautifully. A crescendo
is coming. This is the moment.
This moment, now.

No Music

— Murdoch Burnett

The music
we listened to together
I cannot bear to hear alone. No pain
should be that pure.

No glorious Ninth. No Aaron Copland.
No Gershwin. No Leonard Cohen. No Aretha
Franklin. Do not go dancing.
Pure pain.

I must clean the apartment carefully.
Like a museum. Like a shrine. The sight
of my dishes in the sink moves me to tears.
One wine glass. One plate. As prosaic
as this. Do not forget the cat food.
I say this to myself. Pure pain.
No music.

Watts Towers

— Murdoch Burnett

I want to live like I'm building
Watts Towers. Each moment a glittering
thing to be picked up, a discarded tile
shard from the dust made beautiful
by finding and pressed with love
to the mortar. Then, at the end
of it all, secretly, deep in
me, will be three reaching
towers in bright sunlight.

I have love in me
like the building of Watts Towers.
Each fragment of tile and bottle I find
I will press to mortar with fingers
trembling from that love. I have
love in me like building
Watts Towers.

The fish

— Diana Bryden

You caught that fish like a good fast fuck,
all wet and fishy, all finger sticky.
Gloved in fluids, you tried to unhook him.
Torn by the hook, the fish was sick.
He coughed and shook like a sick old smoker,
he gagged and choked
and you tried to stroke the hook out
but its bright point
sat deep in the wet,
deep in the flesh.
Go deep in my flesh, love, and I'll hold on tight.
I'll loosen when the brightness comes whirring
out of the flesh, shivering and spinning.
Help me, you're calling, *help me hold him!*
The fish in my arms is a desperate baby,
his eyes are wet peas
crinkled and cloudy,
milky with pain.
Milk in the flesh.
He writhes like a baby
and blood spills like urine
in ribbons, in streamers.
He swells in my arms
Till I'm up to the elbows
in fish blood and water.
You can't free the hook,
he thrashes and wrestles,

you bite through the line and he leaps for the water,
trailing behind him a thick spool of whiteness,
the hook still inside him,
the two of us soaked,
hands raw from wetness, cheeks smeared with wetness.
Dig deep my fisherman,
I'll pull you in.

Theft

— Diana Bryden
She walks outside; stone is water, flowing
away from memory. She hears sirens
crying. Set loose, severed
from the ribbons of sight.

Eighty years ago, helping her father
deliver the laundry, she waits with the horses.
His seat beside her, emptied
of him, holds his warmth.
She falls asleep
breathing leather and animal.

I steal small mouthfuls,
a rude bird, snatching from her: *sheets and towels,*
stone-white cotton.

A thief, I fly through the maze
of her memory; dead ends
and tunnels diverging

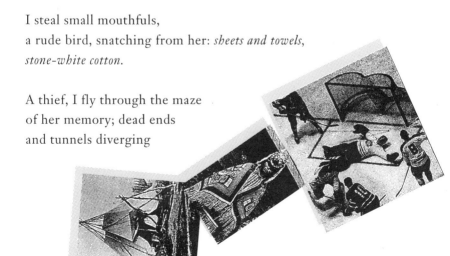

from my purpose: to feed my hunger, but also
to replace lost sight — comfort
with words. Break the stillness
with a sudden flicker
of light, or another small theft.

I was so tiny, I could stand
underneath the horses.
Or they were so big. My head
barely touched their bellies.

Howard Hears Marion Downstairs

— David McGimpsey

I hear you downstairs in the morning.
Your bones are too big; drumbeating out
the sun with their yearning syncopations.

There will be another kind of birdcage for you
and another yellowed Eisenhower era for me;
I hear you downstairs making plans.

You talk out the window to the lanky
brown haired man with crooked, gapped teeth.
You say something that in the movies

would go like this:
"just because I'm a nun
doesn't mean I can forget I'm a woman."

We quiver like chicken hinds
after the voodoo priest has bitten off the head
and its blood forms icicle drips

at the defiant mouth. We shake
like delirious hands, fumbling with a bottle
of Wild Irish Rose by the cold lakeshore.

I hunger for oatmeal that goes right to the blood
and a Messiah with a body like my own
minus the war in Europe,

minus the years of cheap ice cream,
and the rationalization
"maybe if I turned off my tap of Milwaukee's finest."

You are moving our furniture,
at least that's what it sounds like.
Everything is pushed and pulled with railway chugs.

It could be the sound of you scraping
off faded wallpaper; but ours
is brand new and bright as your hopeful trousseau.

Isn't this just like a bruise?
All the purple and yellow anybody could stand
is down there somewhere

amidst the sound of "shh"
and chair coasters rocking against the floor
like hard waves throwing driftwood at the strand.

Porkscraps

— David McGimpsey

He hit me over the head with a shovel
made of soft plastic but I deserved it.
And that, apparently, wasn't enough
I rewrote *The Barkleys of Broadway*

As *Those Magnificent Malignancies*
And got laughed the fuck out of Manhattan.
Oooh ouch I said all the time like a dolt —
I wasn't supposed to be exerting myself.

I wasn't even supposed to mention the weather
to a certain shovel-wielding neighbour;
the big-city guy who looks like Stalin
and claims he's acted with *the* Traci Lords.

"Here's a Tony award for you," he said
before he crowned me the king of New York
and I collapsed in the brown salty snow
just thinking *I really did it this time.*

Shannen Blazon

— David McGimpsey

The last time she threatened me with a .22
we were on the Santa Monica Freeway,
smelling like rich Los Angeles,
pretending to know the mumbled words in popular songs.
It was before the earthquake,
before she picked up that shake in her voice
most noticeable when she says
"I wasn't fired, I quit."
The barrel of the gun was like candy,
I would've held it for her,
still cocked and aimed,
just in case her arm was getting tired.
The central joke was "faster, faster
we've got to get to the Whiskey."
She was all sloppy, like God herself,
out for a spin under the haphazard stars.
She put the thing away and sang:
"Bobbitt-o, Bobbitt-y, boo."

We picked up her friend with the big nostrils
and ended up at the Hotel Mondrian again;
de stijl: straight uncut lines.
I just tried to feel grateful.
Her teeth all crooked in the right ways,
her nose all crooked, her eyes...
She screamed to a makeshift entourage:
"I'll still be in this business

when Christina Applegate is folding tacos
at some dive in Yorba Linda."
She was oblivious to my heart.
She continued her monologue:
"Jenny's just jealous. That's all.
That was *my* book selling in Chicago
and that was *me*, 'the next Bette Davis'
according to that TV critic out in the village there.
How could sweet Jenny's pain,
what with all her bellyflops,
just go away?
That girl will never be alright
until she learns to forgive me
for being a better actress."

Smoking, drinking, but never overeating.
Her leather pants always just so.
Her black velvet smock still very 90210.
The man with the nostrils read from his poems,
something "for a friend at Hazelden."
She had nothing she said but recalled for us all
her final task at the Lycée Français,
to translate a favourite movie scene:
"*J'ai pensée que nous allions au Club Babylon!*"
"*Encore?*"
It was quite impressive, I clapped real loud
and she asked me why I just didn't go home.
I said rough justice was all that I was looking for
not exculpation, not even a promise
to get me in to see her agent.

She gave me $200 and said "get a cab, lady."
The nostril-man laughed.
I said a bunch of things I never said
because I was tired, chastened,
intrigued by the cash.

The Santa Monica Freeway has crumbled now.
The whole city smells like concrete-dust.
I heard the tabloids said it was never meant to be.
They misspelled my name,
but now that's what I go by, professionally.

Time to Wake Up

— Susan Beach
(I am bent over my work
digging out hard, dried earth
over and over I dig the same spot
so tired sore shoulder sore back
but never stop to stretch
— no time —
work is never done
always more
never done always more
to do

I am aware of you
my love bent to this work too
we do not look to each other

— no time —
we are wearing heavy brown robes
I can see barren ground
no more
hoods hide our faces
down in dark openings

a breath of air releases time
to pause   and
in that space
I see:
I am living out
my life
inside the parentheses
of someone
else's
sentence)

Jade

— Christian Bök

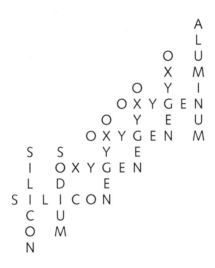

```
                                A
                                L
                        O       U
                        X       M
                  O     Y       I
                O X Y G E       N
              O   Y     E       U
            O X Y G E N         M
        S   S     Y     E
        I   O X Y G E N
        L   D     E
    S I L I C O N
        C   U
        O   M
        N
```

oriental nachtmusik:

opium,
ormolu, alalia.

octagon.

singsong siamang.

origami ouijaboard.

Grain Boundaries

— Christian Bök

```
        rim                     rime
                emery
        memory              remora
        memoir
                    moiré
                                mirror
                                mirage
        image               regime
                gems
        edges               emerge
                energy
        elegy               elegant
                                element
        letter              stellar
        steel
                    steam
                                metal
        master              sleet
                        maelstrom
        icestorm            serum
                        simulacrum
        shimmer             sheer
                        meerschaum
        echelon             mesh
        measure
        muse            machinery
```

Emerald
— Christian Bök

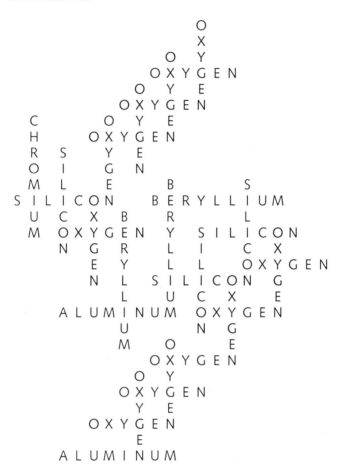

crownland beaumontage:

sidereal
opulence of sinfulness.

opaque, ornate, orphic.

silkscreens of silent
orchards.

oracular silviculture.

alembic of silhouettes:

bezels,
oblique optics.

berylloid observatory.

alkali,
octane, oxides.

ozone overworld of oz.

Commotion

— Gil Adamson

Me here, keeping still,
the family thinking hunt.
A nasty turn of events this morning,
the laundry down there, wet again.

I was waiting to hear from
the local fence-viewer, rain dancer,
perhaps the fat, whiskered bellboy
from downtown.
You know, normal stuff.

But, fuses blew out in the dark hall
and no sun today, just water gushing in.
My mother is jabbing at the coats
in the closet, a pike through hay,
and upstairs I hear my father
swing a chair through the dark,
happy in this ghastly work.

Me? I'm hoping high up was a good idea,
while the river grumbles at its edge
eroding the doorframes, table legs.

Wild State

— Gil Adamson

Now all I do is move.
In the old days, I touched him,
smelled him, dreamed
he burned himself deliberately,
cut himself, a palm-print
in blood across my mouth.

Sometimes, I imagine his head back
on the pillow, arm raised
to cover his eyes,
the wrinkled scar spreading.
Him behind me, fingers
in my mouth.

That phone call I get
at four a.m.
the damp sheets twisted.
I roll to the light
and blast myself awake
to find the line dead.
Take another bath in the dark
and fall asleep
one leg up on the side.

Wake to see the light come up
red against the trucks outside,
black asphalt pooled with rain.

Tracking him like a dog,
seeing his uneven trail
through burnt grass.

But, this isn't the right place
not hot enough,
not empty enough,
the pay phones too upright.

He's out there in the right place
leaning back on a garden chair.
He calls me sometimes
hangs up, calls again.
He can picture me lying in the bath,
half-seeing him, half-asleep.
Sometimes I pay for another day
and stay inside in the dark.

Outside restaurants, I stand
with my hands in my pockets,
watch the parking lot steam.
Morning leaks into the sky.
Legs shaking, I look all the way
down to my boots, step forward.

Listless French Company

— Gil Adamson

Breaking into the reliquary
and eating fish sandwiches by the water
flicking saintly knuckle bones at swans.
Some have lost their service revolvers
and all our sweaters are mossy.
We drink junk and dislike strangers
and walk backwards to erase our worries.
Our ancestry goes back, we feel,
to other planets, the melting of rock,
the big bang.
In several chapters of this great book
we wander into hell and are wiped out.
In other chapters, not so much blood.
We cruise the pages slowly, hiss,
slap each other saying, look here,
it's you dying in this church,
or look now, my horse bit by a snake.
We each see our grim moments,
demented or reeling or severed clean,
see each individual dispatch, our faces
wavering in history's dim flashlight.
We thump the book closed, not believing.

The Church of the Common Cold

— Death Waits

if we can agree that the basis for all religion
is the thesis that mankind is greater
than the sum of its parts
then I propose the church of the common cold
for what else do we share more completely
than the experience of stuffed-up noses
sneezing, coughing and sniffling

services would be held in winter only
a seasonal devotion
Kleenex boxes would line the pews
prayers would be chanted in a clogged, nasal unison
and fever would be the measurement
of one's inherent spiritual worth

for what else do we have in common anymore?
what illusions still stand, what civilized contrivances
can still bear the weight of our tender and sacred need
for hope?...
if I can hear myself sneeze
will it rattle the world?...

I am waiting for spring, when my spiritual practice
can restfully wither
and these jokes made at the expense of humanity
can stare at the sun
and be warmed

Towards a Contentless Society
— Death Waits

it is content that abhors a vacuum
when the dove smacks into the wall
and in doing so is redeemed

content that cannot show its face within the storm
when the split second between stations
becomes the only time allowed for thought

and trying to write the saddest poem
humanity could possibly write
(but what would it contain?) a nothing,
a nothingness: evolution's definition of humanity

my heart is beating faster
than a thousand cracking whips
I bleed from every orifice
and not a single drop of blood
is sacred

In Parking Lots We Lie ...

— Tracy Brooks

In parking lots we lie on the ground
under chevys with thin grins of satisfaction on our faces
frozen blue,
in minus 40 no one cares what your name is or
who you come from.
Pavement fades into frost-ravaged skin
and I am calling you divine.
Divine like a tail-light pulling off into the dark.
Divine like a victim.

In this parking lot hell there are decisions to be made
there are better things to do than recite asphalt psalms under
pickup trucks and family cars
We roll over and imagine your
screams of Jesus are half choking on ecstasy or
half drowning in prayer of resurrection from this
steel and rubber grave.
You cry like a man watching himself burn in gasoline,
like providence has spared your talents on blazing backdrops.
You blend into sheets of saffron like it's a dying profession,
and when you have finished your scene
you are not written back into the script.

On car hoods we sit smoking herbal cigarettes
in the wake of spring

I put your hand between my thighs and laugh,
watching you wash away always did amuse me.
The final scene arrives with speed and deliverance;
you are impatient to begin   as always
your body becomes a misplaced prop
set against the tar
as if a valid point were to be made
upon watching you die.
You never did blend into me.

When the curtain closes we will wrap your body up in it
hide you in the frost,
under the chevy,
beside me.

In this parking lot hell there are bets to be lost.
In conversations there are mentions of names —
those who would love to forget you,
kill you if given the chance,
fuck you if you had the time.
We joke of you falling to the ground
searching for a better salvation than this.
I kiss your face.

In the wake of spring
there is nothing more a pickup truck can offer.

Marking Light

— Tracy Brooks

In this body I have as many bruises as I do bones.
There is enough blood in here to bathe in, 87 scars
marked like light, breaking off into the 3 a.m. night
around me. Studious, I have counted, re-counted
categorized and labelled every wound, accounting
for the faux pas of this life, the brilliancies of others,
leaving a few mystery scars. I figure I probably got
them from carelessness in the womb. Mother probably
stuck a knife in her belly trying to get at the problem or
maybe I was over anxious in my assumption that
great things were to lie ahead, that I was just a
floating object in the greatest space in the universe —
inside another. However, I have no evidence of this
besides belief.

Twenty-three years now. I've tried everything
once. Become addicted to all of it at one time or another.

I read a poem one time about the human
cell — how it can store little pictures of history. In every cell
there is a girl playing skip rope. In every cell there
is a girl being raped or cutting off all of Barbie's hair.
At the ending the girl in the poem collected all those tiny
pieces of herself and lived to become a published author.
I am happy for her.
Sometimes, though, people die of cancer. Had she considered this?
Their cells turn against them — mutiny of sorts.

History kills the momentum. The girl stops jumping.
They turn on themselves.

Every part of a girl commits suicide   one piece at a time.

       Outside of this body, this history, it is May.
The early morning air pours through the open window,
thin, dribbling in with dew on its back. The morning will
come round, sweaty from early-evening foreplay the night
before, but morning is a rarity around here.
This bedroom has been my deathbed, this chair
props up my mortal remains.
Since 2:14 I have been recalling the birthplace of
the scars of my body.
I remember parties, red wine, every nice girl
wearing their bright blue eyes, silver
jewellery catching the light. Doing anything to catch the light.
In drunkenness picking up the pieces of glass,
scarlet stained — reminded me of
my childhood as a catholic.
I remember being over ambitious as a child — falling
out of trees, off of bikes, in front of cars, stuff like that.
In adulthood, we pay to have that sort of thing done.

When history revolts, you have no choice.
Spring hasn't come into full force yet. The
nights still reminisce of winter. It feels more like
autumn on the skin than it does May, like we're
moving back into winter for a second time.

The back of the chair is worn against tight cool
skin. In front of the window, shirt off, my fingers are
following the highways of scars —
roads less travelled. Like stretch marks, they
show where I've been, how I've grown.
The freshest journey, still pink like
a baby's skin. It is warmer than the rest of
the body. It is the most painful of side
streets on my skin.
It's only been a week. I am expected to fully recover.
My left side removed.
I don't want to live to be dependent on my travels,
every morning waking up somewhere new.

3:07
I've been planning where to go from here.
I'll take this ... any direction I'll follow.
Mutiny is the most disgraceful reaction to the present.
Had I known this would happen, I would have
skipped the history part and gotten to the point.
Point being this ...

3:10
I move my hand down from my chest onto the
propped up knee. Bend the wrist down
at a sharp angle ... till it hurts,
till the veins are willing to jump ship with me.
Dressed to occasion, silver jewellery worn
like every cell in my body — loudly.

3:13
I wear this body like burlap, like Nazi leather.
Pink party dress   , built in road map.
This body *is* a road map — Rand McNally
North American Atlas. In a dark room, splashes of
brown, like coffee spills and nicotine,
drowning detroit
duluth
calgary
lethbridge
discolouration blurring the path of one girl's
life with the   tipping of the coffee cup.

3:14
The shadow of silver accessories flashing off,
splintering into little chunks of light,
like plump scars,
thick and unmovable.

   Plug removed from the bath tub, the water pulls
in to gravity.
88 now, none left forgotten or misplaced, however
uncomfortable that is.
88 scars at the age of 23 is the accomplishment
of the rebellious history of the single cell.

The Machine Gunner

— Steven Heighton

I saw them. They came like ghosts out of ground-
mist, moving
over ruined earth in waves, running

no, walking, shoulder to shoulder
like a belt of bullets or like
men: tinned meat lined on a conveyor belt as the sun

exploded in thin shafts on metal
buckles, bayonets, the nodding
spires of helmets. I heard faint battle cries

and whistles, piercing through the shriek
of fire and iron falling, the slurred
cadence of big guns; as they funnelled

like a file of mourners into gaps
in the barbed wire I made quick
calculations and slipped the safety catch.

But held my fire. Alongside me
the boys in the trenches worried them with
rifles, pistols, hand grenades

but they came on, larger now, their faces
almost resolving out of hazed hot
distance, their ranks at close quarters amazing

with dumb courage, numb step, a sound of drugged
choking in gas and green mud, steaming —
Who were these men. I saw them penitent

sagging to knees. I saw their dishevelled
dying. And when finally they broke
into a run it came to me

what they had always been, how I'd always,
really, seen them: boys
rushing toward us with arms

outstretched, hands clenched as if in urgent prayer,
sudden welcome or a reunion
quite unexpected. Yes. And more than this

like children, chased by something behind the lines
and hurrying to us
for rescue —

I spat and swung the gun around. Fired,
felt the metal pulse
and laid them three deep in the wire.

Eating the Worm

— Steven Heighton

Adding up the unfinished, the half-full:

This litre of mescal a friend stowed back for you from Mexico in his
        pickup last Christmas,
This ashtray landscaped with dunes and butts from a second friend
        asleep beside you on the floor,
This gathering for a third friend dead a week now, this wake, this
Grief, you guess it should be, somewhere, something keeps you
        rifling inside for a door that opens inward,
This grief mortared up like a corpse in a concrete wall or the sac that
        sealed round the poison in your father's groin after his
        appendix mined him from the inside and the surgeons only
        found it a year later when they cut him open for something else,
This grief you want to drink your way down to, a swimmer in the
        body's slow locks, or afloat in the bottle descending as the
        level crawls toward the worm,
This grief you know now only as numbness, nonbelief
This grief that like the sac in your father's groin is a pocket of poison
        you've got to uproot, slit open and drain or it explodes,
This grief you would like to explode,
This salt like ashes, sand sprinkled on the arroyo formed of your
        thumb and finger you've got to lick clean before sucking back
This bitterness, as if when you fill yourself with liquor with salt you'll
        feel it flood from your eyes all brine and carry off not only

this guilt but the coffin of your friend, empty, light as a
    shoebox, afloat on the slow locks of the seaway   seaward
This friend who died alone in his house while junk-mail and the
       mail of old friends clattered in through the slot to spread around
       him like a spray of white, fumbled roses, friends passing a few
       feet off in the street friends pausing to finger and smell
       his new-flowering trees, as you did the day he died   as you
       smell and finger now
This worm you've finally reached, poured free, pickled and still, the
       worm you have to eat in some cantina off the road in the
       scavenged Baja in your ribs, your bones, to prove to the patrons
       Yeah you're a man, in your cold white country you can still
       feel still cry the way a man cries or *could* for the one beloved
       friend that each friend is, his body
This whole body racked, in time, as if a mirage out of the desert wind
       is shaking, beating me till I hear it cry out *Why? When I was*
       alive, you didn't — why didn't you love me more, then?
                                        Why?

Long Distance Every Sign

— Steven Heighton

Long distance every sign —
another poem the road gave you.
Another song the aerial
sucked out of sound waves into the car
far gone
on the freeway filed to sand behind your tires
or the forest trail growing in behind you
or the paddles' footprints, fading
in a bay at dawn, as ice knits closed after your stern
and keeps pace —

At the wheel could you feel above you
the sun's wheel turn
and shuttle you into dark, and home — and see
the dashboard's green galaxies at dusk
evolving, burning and by dawn
burnt down

                  (I want to wake at the wheel still driving
somehow changed, want you there beside me
as the road unwires like a heartline, lilting
and we near another elsewhere
want you there at the wheel, at the wheel
I still believe
for as long as it turns
I can clutch the sun I can steer and
brake time to a hold —)

These times I still believe in every poem the road gave me
though at daybreak they shrink away
like a distance every sign, and the road
that seemed by night a bare arm
unbroached by any watch, and reaching
ah, into dawn, emerges

Mondayed —
bone-beige —
manacled with quartz —

                        a scar in the suburbs
of a clock-skulled place.

from Character Weakness
— Judy Radul

Vaguely masturbating against the existing social order against that
filthy fantastic voyage I found myself lying just the way I fell
neglected to run stayed soft white regret wets washes over me. But.

                       •

What is our pleasure in that picture she laughs while he's black is
that his dick her beauty spot so tight and on the next page
theoretical strangulation for longer than eleven inches is right
because our cunt licks it up a pink tongue across the linoleum.

                       •

Aggressive confrontation young men with their tits and ass
hanging out of our skirts so short our balls got rug burn and our
throats were sore from yelling and I told them you know that's not
even what that's for.

•

Cornered coughing crying we faint scream pick up the gun cut him
loose his shirt falls open wondered was that a nipple or just the
shadow of an escape on foot that reverberates in the empty
stairwell.

•

So elemental to bleed every twenty-eight days luminous and
chunky red a relief from the tension and bloating out of the bullet
wound embarrassment when his mother first told him but the man
at the drugstore didn't laugh.

We're quiet because our collection of old ticket stubs and
backstage passes could wipe us out if we believe in it as most
important

•

Pack response our lipstick smudged on the exhaust pipes our
cocks harder than the leather seats never mind the threat of
extinction noble or pathetic our beautiful breasts falling to either
side beneath the ribcages another head of hair.

Leaning against a lamppost on the corner of King and Diversity

— Peter McPhee

flipping a quarter
and trying to decide
which phone call to make
when out from a half star lounge
slips the lost letter of a '63 love affair.
She thinks about crossing
instead meets my eye
asks: do I know what life's about?

Life is about
four feet tall
balding
and a block up the street
turning left
in a rusted volkswagen.

She winks a wide revelation and
leaving an exhaust fume
runs off screaming
follow that car.

Chasing after elusive movement.

I was almost born in the back seat of a moving object.
We made it in time to forgo any legends
and I am named

not after a cab driver
or coincidental officer of the law
but after the solid earth and my grandfathers.

My birth was in the tradition of this civilization
no one looked in my eyes
calling me *Lake of Moons* or
Blue Sea On A Misty Day
and that doesn't bother me
unless looking in the eyes that pass here
naming their children after television
and following that short balding man to the end of the day.

                   •

I have a friend named Sabre
quiet   sharp
a laughing blade
through sunlight
she dazzles

        inspires my direction
through so many choices
to a decision that leans toward
something
        dangerous.

I want to step
into the street
flipping a quarter

risk everything
but the possibility
of at least one more call

to hear someone say
Hey
what are you trying to do?
Get yourself killed?

No

and if I am blindsided
by something as empty
and personal
as *not any more*
I want the bus to
hit me in mid-dream
my eyes wide
so no amount of currency
will close them

a phone booth somewhere
ringing and ringing
my funeral in the back of a cab
at 90 miles per hour
and my body
hurled to a ditch
by the side of the road.

With any luck
I'll still be breathing.

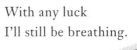

Honky-tonk Angels

— Sina Queyras

Sometimes on Saturdays
my brother and I camped in front
of the t.v. and long after the late show
and popcorn my Mother danced home trailing
the last of the die-hard drinkers from the Legion
down the street and the liquor cabinet was opened
drinks poured as if it were Christmas
the beer nuts came out and I was
sent to spread Cheez Whiz on crackers
pull out gherkins and olives as her
entourage arranged themselves
on the plush chesterfield dropping
cigarette ashes and spilling beer
on the high gloss tables

On these nights there was
always a sing-along
cracked voices and soft
liquid eyes staring up as they sang
and my Mother
the fallen angel choir leader
her cigarette keeping time
sang until the last one had nodded
off or stumbled out
into the early
morning hours

Lily Marlene

— Sina Queyras

In the afternoon we chase
dustballs into corners
swoop upon them with our mop
wash the tiles in a circular motion
square by square until they reflect
our bobbing heads
yours towering
above me

We wash cupboards make beds
precisely tucking corners
and as we feel our way
through the house you sing
Mona Lisa or *The Wedding of Lily
Marlene* and each time you come
to the *tears in the crowded congregation*
I pause as your voice lowers
and in that moment
the slow steady circle of your
sadness becomes me

I could never or could I

— Neil Eustache

I feel like shit.
I wipe the lid of my eye.
Pause to take breath.
There has been this fly.
This one fly that I have been watching for two days.
It's on his back.
For two fuckin days.
The poor fucking thing must be going crazy.
The legs, all six of them just move then stop and then move.
Day in and day out.
The same fucking movement.
I blow smoke at it.
It doesn't seem to care.
Its family, the Fly's family
are all dead.
I scratch my arm and think of laughing or giving some emotion.
To this Fly.
A lamp is near
so is a window, and I see the odd car or truck pass in the distance.
I once tried to find love and happiness and a better set of rules.
I once sat in bed for two days, sober and cold penniless.
It's a couple of days past remembrance day.
Two poppies hang from my curtain.
The Fly, I will call it *Legs*
is half as sane as I am.

The last few great ideas ended up to be a crock of shit.

"Should I kill Legs?"
Naw, it's good to see something suffer less than yourself.
I think and the only reason is?
I am but a simple human, Jesus.
I can really get depressed.

or class and race

— Neil Eustache
same small drugs
they smoked last year
when will legalization
be a nightmare
death to the overpaid
the underpaid
the paid and the cocksucker who killed my dog
death to the
serious
the tattoos
the men carry their babies across the border
Christianity hasn't done enough
I believe in death
as a cure for the rise in hatred
Jesus, You know better
as a cure for almost anything
we kill in our group,
or class and race.

Fred Johnson,
computer engineer
25 years with the company
married
never late in his life
retires next month
full pension and a spot on the wall

I ask you
the garbage men, mail woman, the crooked, the lame, the over
sexed, the nonpaid
do you hate Fred like I do?
never a dull moment with old Fred Johnson,

until that day at the home
when he finds his wife fucking
the next-door neighbour's dog

the poor fucker
25 years
working at the same shit job
living with the same shit wife
and there she is fucking the dog

I don't care
is that what you think?
when you read this
just think for yourself
just think for yourself

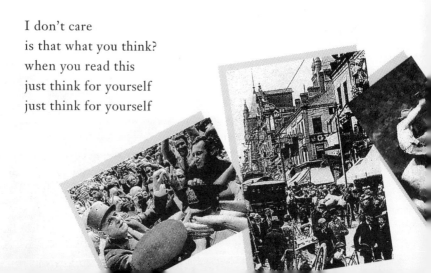

Fred Johnson is my little pet name for poetry
the wife is the paper
and the words are the dogs
and don't you feel a little fucked now?

I don't care

Life Boy

— Susan Helwig

That's my Mom out there under the lilac tree talking to the man
in the brown felt hat with the big black car that's so hot in the
sun it hurts my fingers to look she's going to trade me to him
for a new oilcloth to put on the kitchen table the old one is
smooth but has no pictures left   a new one with bright colours
she doesn't want me now that there's a baby boy in her tummy
that I felt when we took a bath together Saturday night in the
tub that smelled like pine needles and steel when my Dad
brought it in from under the tree by the pump house and we
used the green soap from the Avon lady but sometimes it's an
orangey-red soap, *Life Boy* Mom calls it and it's like the boy
she's got inside her and then I bite my lip where the skin is dry
and crackly from my baby teeth that aren't growing in right and
I know she's always talking about having a baby boy I can hear
her even when she's not saying anything just like now with the
man beside his big black car as smooth and shiny as her tummy
that smells like baby powder and salmon from a can that she
makes when company comes and I know she's giving me to the
man for a new oilcloth even though I'm stuck at the table in my

high chair watching the little puffs of wheat float in a big bowl of milk and now I've got some milk in my hair and it will smell bad and sour until the next time I take a bath and I'm not out there beside his car but I can hear him thinking about me beside the telephone pole like a shaggy tar bear that's too big to hug she doesn't want me anymore the bathtub is getting too small for both of us and the boy.

If you are sad

— Susan Helwig

If you are sad tonight, do not write it down
nothing ends a party faster than a hurting song
do not imagine the candle wavering with emotion
while you turn the bathwater red
vertical slashes mean you're serious
he once said, as if you needed technical advice;
do not grab Death by the back of the neck
& try to kiss him
he is not a lonely twenty-three-year-old who needs a friend
if you are sad tonight, no one wants to know
leave quickly in a cab & watch it scar the new-fallen snow
all the way home.

Who Is Luis Possy

— Dennis Denisoff

I mean besides dead. First cutting
(as if dissecting)
and then eating his words:

> We are being pushed to the
> brink. A little given, and
> a little something waiting.
> We are pushed, pushed ie:

come here you slimy chronofage:)

Unbreakable Combs For Men

until the king of Egypt saw his own frail son
pass before him as a prisoner

to lay you on your back and deep pump you until
hot flick of a back lash

so then ie: EI EIO where
   E equals moments of credence
   O equals moments of release
   Egypt as a square shadow of Eden
   (Frowned ewe's brow, having eaten

re: rereading the tableau vivant
come skulking
all his friends around him

frail, lamenting and releasing
(one spreads its wings
and they all do)

AIDS AS ACCESS TO INTIMACY

the light just so
chicken mesh of punctuation
(as opposed to the excitable
"This poem just dances rings around the grammar!"
(here a conscious of, there a conscious of

> a squint of green
> water-skiers in red
> swimsuits over the
> wakes

any poem has two enemies one
internal one external to
the text as over the weeks
death becomes a source
(up the staircase on his ass for example crying)

Luis or as my grandfather says.   Luis.
his embarrassingly depraved
lips flailing
furious
as intimate as a weakness
the masses not concerned but curious

break grief away from the voice
words as poison or perfume
depending on where you put them
he sure as fuck well

the elements and not the kettles (of course
how as you well know by now already of this design and how

"Hey waiter, I didn't order this.
Who ordered this and who brought it to *me*?"

My hand resting nearby
so that if he should decide or need to

the interior design supports
no design is owned
poetry is no longer something on the plate

> Possy's words become carnivores: Word off
> word. Image off image. Sunny side up.
> Grease as ease. Healthy as maggots. Success
> to the death (and always always St. Theresa's
> amber glow). Vulturous as anteaters.
> Somebody else's babies

lay him on his fetal side and straddle his hip firmly
as a saddler
first in Egypt
then in Nanaimo

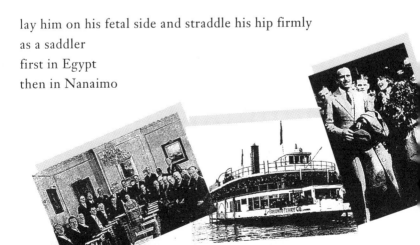

pecs like car roofs

perhaps related to this remark is
the concept behind
the frail ancient painter's coffee round ass and soft curls

visibility to rough fuck
the masses as decisively derisive
up to one's elbows in it.   Luck.
delicacies
and soft curls of cheese
and capers and onions
and a whole done ham to gnaw on

> We want life since greed is chronological:
> edacity, esurience, gluttony, gormandizing,
> see insatiableness, see ravenousness, see
> voracity, see voluptuousness, see hunger

this pain here
that itch
this prolonged desire to
eat to
desire to
vomit
the masses not solicitous but obsequious

in desperation
on the death bed
the sky becomes more and more

Italy
this pale blue ancient failure
for you, I'll try:

bulldog
blue

the sun conched in the shell of ear
the crease on the lobe
the chrome on the tub

heaven shadows Egypt
some are jealous because fags are not
as ageless and instant as coffee
in a proper copper nipple

Aztecs burying their dogs
(but not the Spaniards
mother says don't let him bleed (on your white shirt or open wounds
"fags just eat and eat and eat and eat and eat and eat and eat and

eat

dreams laid on palms like unwanted fish
possum fetus
chewing each other in contempt
too much cleanliness and dry will
runny breathing

(I remember this later and work it in)
a gentle tug through a sure fog
a gentle fag whose dense grey hair

but when a few days
afterward one of Al
exander's own men c
ame to die, hairles

St. Paul S
t. Theresa
step out o   with a   s and helpless, par
f the bath   ll thi   ted, the cold windo
water (luk   s know   w sucking heat from
e warm) an   ledge,   his grey cheek, his
d shake on   who wo   eyes flaring like f
it   uld wa   aghens barely aware
    nt a y   of the sepulcher, o

a rabid spaniel's mouth clamps over the king, then he
    amp, n   , the king, at last
    o just   was wary and just o
    a sand   r not simply so but
    box fi   sad and filled with
    lled w   unleashed remorse
    ith an

entire Vienna boys choir
lashes out to here and o

Graze

— Margaret Christakos

Blades on frozen lake elide her anxieties
about rarely seen friends, relatives, she'd rather
skate until dinner bells
thrash frost's amphi/
theatrical silence

As soon as winter's miracle
of breath   bright outside herself, puffy & close
comforts enough for december
                              january
                                    february
Grace recuperates her high skates to whiteness —
        vinegar to lift salt from the boot tops
        soft shammy to encourage tongues out of hiding
        runners ground to a glint
        new laces keenly yanked —

& each saturday, stakes her balance on one blade's front teeth
a ballast dug into ice, seeking the stroke that's launched
a thousand hips, then *finds* it, & pitches through in a forward motion
removing snow from her path like a long scarf, flamboyant
strip/   tease of the sole
like Magnusson gone to the ice capades

        stroke glide stroke
        thighs pump to inner tracks *this is not*

a "Puppy Love" this is
a snow job uncovered, bliss
of surpassing her
missing self etched
then lost again

well, after gold what's left but
scissor strokes to the rear: perfectly good lines crossed over
                           whited out, her odd jour-
knee
     tucked & chin up, Grace chases her fingers to the tip of nightfall
as if her future grazes at the rink's underside
a dervish magnet pulling from beneath
that keeps her figuring past herself
& the present's unmarked finish line

At least in this routine
she loves these circles of scintillant privacy, gravity
she gives herself leave of,
                leaps over

     (wordlessness,
     that double axel)

                     & glides back to
one beginning or another

* Karen Magnusson, Canadian, Ladies' World Figure Skating Champion, 1973.

Special Effect

— Margaret Christakos

It buries its face in Grace's soft, warm neck
holding itself in the space of a kiss
where it doesn't belong, then pulls back
& says you are loved

now at a distance
it undresses, undoes the pants
& oversweater, slips out of, off it
but as it leans forward
below shirttail is the cock
long vertical excess
pointing straight down like a rope
the body floats above

& Grace's eyes fill up with its excessiveness
in that space, with those words

where the tongue is sent to penetrate
it would penetrate

Then it adjusts the whole body
notices how its tongue is outside itself
how it's swollen at the head
puffy with how outside it is
& tries to push it back

inside the underwear slit: <u>ampersand</u>
men can remain dressed behind
while the tongue exposes itself
a band of bareness
high stake between Man & Space
erected in the frontier
of her *body*
crosscut by
her *vision*
full with consequence
with language,   full
patertongue

An Infant Rhesus Monkey Left Alone Will Die

— R.M. Vaughan
is a useful experiment
for undergraduates — it teaches them humility

3 cages — baby monkey with mother (infant thrives)
       baby monkey with wood and cloth replica (stunted growth,
       heart-warming mugging)
       baby monkey left alone
          (will die and it's all on tape somebody watched his tiny deat
          unfold ... did nothing   after a week   the monkey
          sleeps fitfully, eats nothing, paces paces paces   then stop
          curls into a ball)

please, intervene   you got the point just open
the box   pull him out his mother's only two cages down
youbastardyoubastardyoubastardyoubastard

3 rooms — me with large man who loves me unconditionally (we get a dog
          together)
          me with indifferent but cute guy (i love him unconditionally,
          we kiss in the photobooth at Eaton's)
          me left alone
(sleep just fine   eat — Jesus yes i eat   pace pace pace
myself at the bar   then stop
my   fists   curl into balls)

The Instructive Body Raag (1)

— R.M. Vaughan

how word
        of mouth   is a circular phrase

like   iron-fisted   or   boy   next   door   if broken up
in the longest, even Proustian, paragraph
        messed over like Search-A-Word   they
find each other   make unlikely subsets

I once had a behaviourist shrink who circled
every angry word in my poetry

so many yellow highlighter loops, like spilled Cheerios
words I didn't know were there but
pretended I did   because his next question was do you hear voices
and I almost lied

discontent and its society (10)

— R.M. Vaughan

remember that when you ask me how my parents deal   or
don't I ever worry about   or
how old was I when I knew
questions you couldn't ask   a married son, a woman with three
    children
    a boy of twelve

but you can — I've fucked one, met the other, been the last

Adam and Steve did exist
Satan couldn't bejewel Steve   he knew gold was not the right colour for
perpetual midsummer   (now, if the apple had been white ...)
as for Satan's charm   Steve was Created yesterday (but stayed up
all night)

Satan failed   to sing open the Sky of Knowing
'cause once Steve met God, social climbing was no longer an issue

Satan told HimSelf   I don't care but do they have to do it in front of me
shove it down my ten-foot throat?

and God smote Steve in the west garden
where all the flowers took their names from operas yet written or
George Cukor movies

and Adam, looking up, up into the unchanging, tiresome sky
understood why God made only one of everything

The Fall

— **Mary Cameron**
In the sky sails by Daniel Boone's coon hat
in a fast high wind from the south

and my mouth sore from breathing and winter
coils in my skull, freezes solid for weeks

and my cheeks, too, sting with a northerly
dread of it. So unarmed for cruel weather

I descend into what I imagine a dream:

the clouds only hang there, still as
a painting of the new world. Constable is

skying with a pleasure that ignores
any break in the mind; in the skin or bone

there could be no bleeding. All we're seeking
is a warm light, even dying. The cold wind —

you know, *dead men naked* — grabs us from below.

Apple

— **Mary Cameron**
Every bite I take of the green
apple is tainted with dread: the wizened
entry on the other side, the tiny
brown hole. My teeth sink in, and I
examine what is left, expecting
a body, colourless, to stand out
from the flesh. What shouldn't be there.
I watch your face every morning
with amazement. You drive me
to the edge of the cliff the road takes
a swift turn away from. When I
foolishly lean from a window
you hold all my weight.

Hunger

— Mary Cameron

I drew you, lines of your soft cock
and my single, separate hand.
              Each finger crooked

upward, open palm.
Asleep you were a child, dreaming,

while across the lake a small boy called
to his father, *I'm doing it, can't you see?*

splashing water, brief applause
for the afternoon.

              Your face turned
at the small voice, waking
into a flat, lost apparition.

Night

— Joe Blades

With insomnia this night
like January ice fading
in a warmer than ever January thaw
The valley and town filling
with soft warm fog

Feeling invalid again
Almost fall asleep
while writing in bed (don't ...)
and unexpected tears run
reluctant down my stubbled cheeks

The art and the words
Fear of and love
confusion and reluctance
what I am   What I believe
I am almost capable of

Tired   Tried but unable to fall
into night's ease so writing
Drinking Red Dog beer
Naked but for a jackshirt
Wondering if I am mad enough

What am I thinking?
What can I hope to do?
A monkey with crossed legs
too twisted to "hang loose"
My image in the mirror obscure

1:45 a.m. and someone is knocking
on a door down the hall
Once they enter or leave
I will dress again
and walk with the night

Out into a surprising iciness
A glaze of drizzle coating the road
and cross-ties of the nine spans
of the meditation railway bridge
and the Japanese temple bridge

Walking the ties like climbing stairs
Watching each foot's slippery step
River ice white far below
not that I could ever fall
through the narrow cooing of pigeons

Walking The few moving cars —
taxis and police — sound mystic
and the transport trucks loom
out of the mist like enslaved elephants
resigned while I slip along their paths

If I simply go back to my room
to my not-monastic-enough cell
I will have to aim to sleep
like the arrows of mischievous cherub
when insomnia is my only companion

All coffee shops and restaurants
are closed Only a gas station open
thick with cabbies and no tables
No place to sit and write
So I continue walking Walking

The Dogs

— Joe Blades

The dogs are restless
straining at their leashes
their chains
their domesticated masters

In the mosquito and dryfly night
fireflies flashing their *here i am*
in the grass alongside the endless river
The dogs pulling people along the shores

The dogs know me
living in the approach of darkness
I am here always
without electric body chemistry

The steel blue-black river
breaks white with a leaping salmon
The air smells bladesian
with lightning from beyond

River stipples with scattered raindrops
Dogs sniffing me out
but not lifting their legs
to claim this bench

The dogs read over my shoulder
as I try writing tonight
They thrust their heads in my hands
The dogs already own me

Harmonic Rasp

— Mary Elizabeth Grace

You play a *czardas*
with that hand
those two fingers half gone

that the child in me says never belonged

except
to some black and white photograph
in some history book
about some war
that
has never
lived
in my head

will we ever sit
at the same kitchen table
agree
the pain they caused you
equals
the pain you caused me

it doesn't matter
it's all red
it's all mixed blood

it's just you and I
you playing your harmonica

the grey now coming into your dark hair
the grey now coming into your dark eyes

and there is no answer for the weeping
that's still asking why

czardas — a Hungarian dance with a slow start and a quick, wild finish.

from Loveruage

— Ashok Mathur

Yes, there you were, standing there in pose as if you had always been standing there, statuesque sorrow, waiting for my arrival. And so damn beautiful. So beautiful no words could ever touch the truth you told to me, that day, standing there alone and sorrowed. Yes, there you were. And I came to you unspeakingly and touched your shoulder, cold, and pulled your eyes. And so we met.

That day, that was such a day, we met and never said a word. I did not know what I mistook for thoughtful air, a wordlessness that came from you, was not a fact of silence but of volumes written out to you, on you, in you. And we walked in this word-filled silence down a thousand misty bridges into morning fog and we had steps of children and of each other. We walked to each other's stride, carefully, and always so unspokenly. I began to fabricate a story, my story, which after hours became the true story, of how your vocal chords were lost so long ago and words meant nothing to you now, words were only spaces to fill the power of your silence, and you would not bow to that. My story had you vowing yourself into quiet, leaving the hard-edged, crisp-toned world that I had known as home, and taking yourself away to a world that knew no sound, no language, no voice.

And I knew I was right. And you let me believe so. And then you let drop the sorrow from your eyes, and in a moment of unbelievable light, lips still unparted, you took me into your sound.

"Blood."

"WHAT?"

"( )"

"You spoke. You spoke. You said. You said blood?"

"( )"

"You did. I thought you couldn't speak. But you said blood, I know you did, I heard you say it, Ohmygod, you spoke. Say it again, please? What did you mean, 'Blood'? That's what you said, isn't it? It is, tell me it is."

But your face was back into itself again, and there we were, standing there, facing each other, me snapping word after word at you, and you with your eyes hidden by the shadow of your brow, stone-still and saying nothing. We were like that for ages, hours, yes, I'm sure. Me fumbling for words that were covered over by silence, and you, one word escaping, living with the words covered by your shawl.

I watched you. And I loved you. Then, if not before, before we began our walking over bridges and into misty mornings. For certain then. And so your hand came out from under that earth-grey shawl and seemed to move without your body to brush back the shadows from your eyes. And I saw. And your hand moved across the surface of your body, down past chest and belly and hip, and with a gesture that was not there, touched without touching between your legs.

"Blood."
"Blood?"
"Blood."

I did not wonder, then, as perhaps I should have, whether the blood you spoke was the flow of your body or the unnatural loss from a wound. You spoke without sorrow or joy. You spoke your blood as the body speaks. And your blood and your voice touched my ear and mind with a softness which made me not question who you were or from where came your blood. I only listened to your blood and heard your hand sweep down and in

touching yourself engulf my body too.

And as if we knew each other's bodies, if not words, we turned to search out more bridges.

This was a dream to me, my love, your body come into mine as a dream. Your blood flowed inside me and warmed me and pulsed me. And when the time came, when you stopped, stared, and began laughing deeply, I laughed too, and I did not know why, but I knew I was right to laugh. So, together, our throats gurgled and our diaphragms heaved and we sank to the wet pavement uncaring for our clothes or our bodies, laughing. Your hand rose again, again not part of your body, but always part of you, and you pointed to the building we sat beside. The mist was heavy now and I could see only a grey outline in a grey evening. The building was square, consistent, a block of grey ever so slightly darker than the surrounding mist. A huge brown grey centre marked its doorway, oaken and shut. And your finger pointed.

"This is the sky."
"The sky?"
"The sky. This is."
"This church. Is the sky.?"
"This, the sky."

And your arm, still outstretched, finger pointing as if in accusation, went taut and frozen, and I read the sky in your hand. Did we rise and walk, or did the mist carry us? We were inside, and your arm was still raised in salute to the sky, and all around us were oak pews.

"Pebbles to the sea."

I would have sworn the pews themselves trembled to your words. We were the only sound in the church which I knew for certain was the sky. And the pews were now pebbles to the sea. There was no other choice. Pebbles to the sea in the sky and your words were never clearer. Floated: you did, you floated down the aisle to the altar, although I knew better than to call this an altar. I waited for your words. You surveyed the scene, eyes passing over a stained pulpit to the crucified sculpture hanging above. I knew your words were a judgement and a naming and I knew I would never not understand again. Your shawl slipped off your shoulders and a cruel pink glow blew from your back, words stunning me with their force, glancing off me with their brilliance, sinking into me with their sound. You wore a thousand words inside your skin, and I knew they were not your words but would always have to be your words. You had been named and unnamed so many times a palimpsest was where your skin should be. And so, the words already screaming from your body, you began to speak to, to name, the figure on the cross.

Going to the Eyestone
— Deirdre Dwyer

The texture of this

When you come out
of the Christmas craft market
on a quiet day that began with coffee
and muffins you remind yourself
that today's Sunday, not a day of routine.

You come outside:
a man is selling apples,
his truck parked behind him,
boxes of apples at his feet.
It's the hour before dusk
when the air is not dark yet
but almost a silver colour
like birchbark
and it's snowing
the kind of snow that almost
turns to rain

But doesn't.
This kind of snow
made of thin needles of silver.

This kind of snow — or is it a rain
of fireflies dancing off your face? —
so precarious, so careful

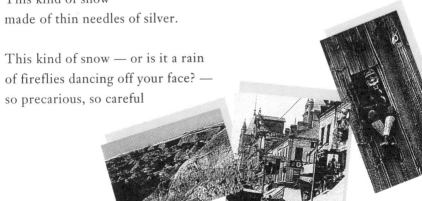

you wonder if all the craftsmen
are dazed
by what you can know
only by touch.

The Breath that Lightens the Body

— **Deirdre Dwyer**

Coming inland

You can't know the mind-drifts,
the dreams between sentences,
conversations between mind-spins,
somersaults brought about by Singha beer,
magic mushrooms, grass,
Mekhong and Cokes.

But when can I come inland?

Every time I try
someone offers me a hit
reiterated around the table
in a slur and mumble of words.

When I say dream
I mean meditation in a hot season
                    of salt spray and wind.
Josh, a wise-knows-the-waters kind of guy,
when he says fishing he means patience.

His renovated Chinese junk from Singapore,
his quiet brown Sri Lankan smile.
You can come inland anywhere

Or you can go out to bays,
private white beaches,
anchor down through
clear water to coral.

It's not so much where you are
but how to get there.
Not where do you want to be
but why or why not.
Not when or which intense lifetime,
but meandering between delta and inlet,
water and land.

Phase II

— Valerie Hesp

Look she said
Look at this
Go past the first layer
See revealed Obvious Irony
Keep going
Look at how hard
It is
That we've worked to get
At where we are

Look beneath
Peek under the cover
What's opened up for you?
What do you see?

I see the effort, yes,
But that's only a part
Their covers cover only part

What else is it?
What else is there?

Some iron strength
Some strong metal
Some copper anger
Smouldering softly
At the Core

And when you come to me
I am speechless
Quiet
How can I say
It's not my conversation
It's not my Time
You're on your own
You are

I see the ripples
After the original stone
Thrown loudly into the pond
Where we are

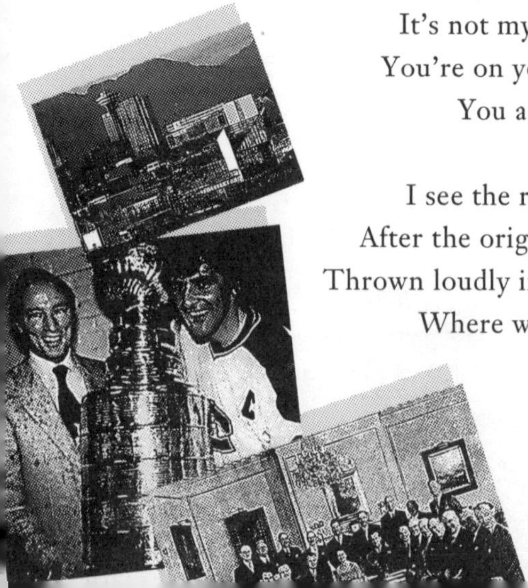

Gilbert Cove, Nova Scotia

— Valerie Hesp

This day of Light
quick air
large shape, round & square
tiny pebbles, uneven —
Expands my presence
so I merge
with shifting mist

& Dance
Away ....

Bugs, Snakes, and Snow

— Stan Rogal

In the movie
Molly Ringwald plays Betsy
And Tom Cruise plays Ike.
Amazing combination
        who earlier might have been Monroe and Mitchum.
The bugs are impressed.
The snakes are impressed.
Even the snow ends its swirly drift to take a peek.
Except, in the film,
        there are no bugs, no snakes, and no snow.
This having less to do with artistic licence
        and everything to do with box office

the bugs, snakes, and snow
            laugh up their sleeves, thinking,
    Wouldn't Betsy and Ike have loved that?
Also, Molly and Tom are an extremely cute couple.
They wear cute prairie outfits.
They speak in cute Canadian accents.
The dirt on their hands and faces is cute.
They have a cute dog
        and the wagon is drawn by two real cute horses.
Where are them dumb oxen? wonder the bugs.
Where's that Shanghai rooster? wonder the snakes.
Where's that spotted hog? wonders the snow.
That's not all.
Molly and Tom discuss everything together.
In one scene Molly saves the life of the Indian Chief's son.
In another scene Tom cries.
This is a very progressive movie.
In the sex scenes Tom is always shown in underwear.
The underwear is clean and Tom (we notice)
        (almost naked) is, really, too cute for words.
Molly, also, is, really, too cute for words.
Her breasts, bare, are the perfect size and shape.
Not too big, not too small and so
        well behaved. Her nipples,
                perky, without being obnoxious,
        strike a fine family-viewing line between the
Erotic and the pornographic.
Someone has done their homework
        and the lovemaking scenes are quite honestly

cute beyond measure.
Naturally, they arrive on the West Coast
None the worse for wear
and proceed to amass a fortune
selling lumber to the Brits
to build ships
So that Nelson can defeat Napoleon.
The final shot is the presentation of medals
against a painted backdrop of giant pines
while the bugs, snakes, and snow
split a gut off-stage
rolling among the
stumps, slash, and
Ashes.
Cute, they think. *Very cute!*
Who'd've thunk
A comedy?
And that's the end of the movie.
That's the end of
It.

She Evaporates with Drops of Water Flung from her Hair

— Louise Fox

In the very middle of a lawn like astroturf
is a tan house with pink trim.
Inside, polyethylene covers the plaid chesterfield and chair set;
A high-gloss coffee table has been wiped again,
along with the empty TV face.

The kitchen floor shines hard as new teeth.
And in the bathroom a shower curtain crisply hides
  a towelled-out box of whiteness.
The not-too-lush African violet sits on one end of the
  master bedroom's knickknack shelf beside a white china poodle
  whose little red eyes are dusted every day,
  after the 8x10 school pictures are done.

The family are going out for a slow Sunday drive and swim,
  with a nice full tank of gas.
The thoroughly washed back seat only slightly sticks to
  the legs and underpants of the children.
Halfway down the driveway, father stops to gather
  a few pieces of gravel spat on the grass from his
  cautiously turning wheels.

They pass the clean edge of their lawn.
Out of the ditch sprawls a wild rose,
  unruly, full of perfume and bugs;
And on the shoulder of the road a grove of queen anne's lace
  indifferently shades a broken bottle and a mud-flattened
  cake wrapper.
Between two birch trees, larch rush out to grab the light.
Chewed and battered spruce bunch together in a wall, beyond which
  shines the layered changing sea.

Mother worries dust is flying through the windows.
Father thinks of a gumwrapper in the ash tray:
  Empty now? Or wait?
The heat and swarm of flies, and a seagull dropping feces

on the windshield sicken them all a little.
They want to go home and eat porkchops and microwave frenchfries
    and a small hill of peas on their corning-ware plates.

At the sea there are floppy purple jellyfish,
    rolling side to side;
And crabs shoot off randomly.
The sea is slow and long, but so very big.
The deep cave of it is so near,
    where giant mouths suck and pull in the dark blue,
    and there are no rules.

Mother, up to her knees in water, aches with fear.
    The kids screech and dash with some others.
    Father sits on a clean towel with the radio.
She waits and waits, her hands in front of her,
    warding off the great crushing chaos,
    her heart like a sharp stone.
She takes a rigid dive, keeping her head up — no salt
    water on her hair.
But when she turns, a wave gobbles behind,
    bubbling her into shore.
She flings herself backward.
The sea's between her legs and under her eyelids.
She whirls around and dives,
    and up,
    and dives again.
The world's no longer clear and neat, but a wet, stinging
    uneven marvel.
She evaporates with drops of water flung from her hair.

Inventory

— Lise Downe

Eight sky scenes improvise an evolution of soothing
geometry awash in yellows, oranges, purples,
and blues suggest a blue field unfolding
nervously inside a room of creamy whites.

Two icons on the too-big lawn amplify
and separate
their complex of lopsided shutters
balanced by an undulating wave.

Your eyes   your hands
initially perceived as a refuge
extend like smaller squares
into the storm of panelled doors.

A line of black and white dots
the landscape.

      this place acts as a skylight
      these floors channel the ceiling
      the right angles oooh and aaah

Private indulgence in the midst of
their vernacular   their abiding and formative spectrum
perched with
          unsentimental directness
even cubist
the tidal wave's splash of red

spilling sassafras onto the checkerboard.
This succession of s's ascending
as though magically twisted or wrought iron from long ago
had made a come-back
only to serve as an end-table
in this palatial hut.

Nomad

— Lise Downe

the leaf handles a precarious lily
juggling preamble with suggestive vowels
measured words for the nondescript
         the photograph
         the phonograph playing
broad daylight in an unfamiliar bed
one has to invent:
            conversation
            commotion

loose sheets blown into the top branches

      apples

               free falling

      there

as long as the ground circles
that same freckled streetcar will deflect
    the question:

Does this *seem* strange?

the silver door pushed open
      revolves or depends largely
      depending on rapidly
      repeating
a word or phrase five or six times
in quick succession

a guttural arrangement of canyons and
                        cliffs
casting long shadows
          through the peculiar light
              singing sweet underground
singing eloquence into murmuring

a single *impression*
               of
                  daybreak

      turquoise sky

white petals drift slow loris

turning leaf to feather
      the mysteries
      like human hands
      have it
      so pat

Asphalt Cigar

— Kevin Connolly

O, the heartbreak!
The mean transistor,
the incontinent sponge of faith.
An hereditary passing
from parent to offspring —
you were born with these relations,
mental leaps, associations:
the militant thugs,
the multilingual polyglots.

The bridge over this city
specializes in heavy transit:
trucks and vans carrying
baked goods, trucks delivering
other trucks and vans ...
The city is swollen with
a defeat many years in the making.
Each lung has its bachelor apartment.
Nothing crosses over.

You've been falling slowly
through the faltering air.
Ever since you were born
you've been falling
into this lifelike sink,
oiled and swirling,

overlooked by roaches
and luxury motor lodges.
At last the way jumps clear
into your greasy lenses.
I might even let you follow it —
time's syncopated sludge drum.
Ju jubes, glop, an ardent
prayer: the sum-trickling
wealth of civilization
lies ogling your spirited feet.

Order Picker

— **Kevin Connolly**

Category Four: Horsemanship

I lose a broken watch,
then dream I am my father.

Category Twelve: Fidelity

The python licks
the cold mirror.

Category Seventeen: Faith

A group of flightless birds
admired by thieves.

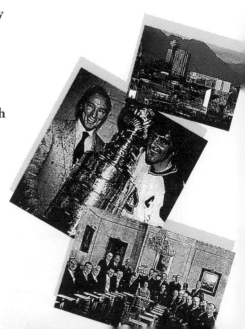

Category Eighty: An Anecdote

I invent a strange instrument,
motorless and unassembled.

Category Seventy-Six: Advancement

The black hill; a heavy cloud
grasps its own unfolding.

Deathcake

— Kevin Connolly

What I wouldn't give for something
really juicy right about now —
a piece of *contemperobilia*,
garnished with some lightweight surrender
for the closing and in the meantime
a gruelling scene or two: rabid chucksteak
in the warehouse of slim pyjamas.

Instead, another entry for *The Concise
History of the Literary Buttocks*,
Chapter Two: Cracksweat and Saggy Trousers.
If you don't have a bubo a good
scab will do. You see, all I ever
had was this deathcake, an itchy ballpoint
& a bouquet of wounded toes.

Mother's Milk

— **Jenny Haysom**

Your heart is low percussion — a swab
clubbing your chest. Sometimes I imagine I have grown
inside you; nine months, twelve months, twenty months! Drawn up

by the primal beat, I reach that space
behind your breasts, the pink
mould of ribs and flesh, a well-worn chair.

Mother, in my vocabulary, you mean
reliable, familiar. At night, the turn
of laundry reminds me you are folding

warm sheets, or washing dishes; up to your elbows
in mother's milk. I am sad to say
I love these things about you.

And still, my sleep is stitched by the quick
needle of your sewing-machine, paced
by the rhythms from your upper arm (though in this dream

you stand beyond the door, watching
the breath in my nightdress, a slumber
sprigged and familiar).

Yellow Curtains

— Jenny Haysom

Resting in hospital gowns,
curtained off, that same yellow cloth.
And all the knees trembling
numb, as if humming
up from our soles some far-off
close construction site.

The reasons feel so pointless.
A fourteen-year-old rubbing the blood
back into her glass toes. The mother
of eight who cups her ears
to the silence. And me —
I am the yellow cloth that opens
in the back, that flees
on steel runners and traces the track
of an unlined, unborn palm.

Indian Summer

— Michael Redhill

Summer with its smooth body
recurs like a dream. It has
the beautiful energy of women.
During our first winter
it never stopped snowing.
Its shadow fell across our faces.

As sometimes I go mad
for the love I miss, so everything
must reach back. The indian summer
is pity, gone love returning
its music far off, but remembered
as all our pasts, as certain
as drinking water.

Like the space made
between first finger and thumb
we can bring it back
over and over. So we recall
the scent, the sense
of the space we loved in,
grew warm in, disappeared from.

There is little difference
in the shape of a hand
against your face, and the same hand
empty.

Mergansers

— Michael Redhill

Fat and green and black, duck-thick
they move slowly through the grass,
drawn to the reflecting pool.
Spinning seed pods helicopter
and sink under the diamond surface
where they become sleek schools of minnow,
moving sharp as a single thought.
Everything that loves to live comes here,
to the edge of water, even though it changes
those who gaze or move through it.
It's an unhappy element, chained to itself, vanishing
at the edge of its own membrane. Mergansers
who puddle up through the greeny-blue
are devouring the space they came from,
and above them, we see our solid bodies
waver, two broken skins meeting —
an illusioned space. It's food and fire,
oxygenated earth, everything that returns:
the man reading a paper on the bench,
the ducks eating plugs of soil in the grass.
It's this paper and this hand. It's as unfree
as any free land.

Outside Québec City

— Michael Redhill

The two brothers were huddled in the VIA seat,
the elder's eyes going click click
over Québec fields. The eight-year-old
watched me write a letter, his fingers
zigzagging a mimicked alphabet into his hand.
He had a Micmac face, a tiny cat's head.
I asked him where he was from, he said
it was a grey house with a banana tree. Not Micmac.
He put his head down and closed one eye
making me vanish, then come back. What do you like
about your house, I ask. He bolts up,
chirps *candy*. I ask him what he likes least
and then he's silent. You like everything, I say.
The elder is watching me in the window:
He no like tear gas.

Now we sit quietly and dusk is coming.
The one brother has told me everything.
The little one plays quietly with my travelling clock.
We clack over the tracks to the townships:
Bogota Bogota Bogota Bogota.

Extra

— Karen Mac Cormack

Five mock candles in the chandelier. Your proof's my first floor to ceiling window. Ribbons and bows cross branches on the drawers but sense of smell hesitates. The chili suspended. Raised sidewalks, paved-over dust, grill-work replicated on condensation. Swilk repetition exceeds liftoff. Placebo mention included here as 'entry.'

Benches in the text moments of repose, signatures, shawls and levels respect cloth. Plumage remote. Gems at hand that over please. To meet increased demand there's no discussion only monologue. Ironing (literally) to get the kinks out. Woven, unravelled, rehearsed to point tedium. Occupation as a place to be. Every day's journey.

No root or mainstay, nor slippers to shoe repair, the domestic animal's without leash. Render dollars to satisfy expetible. The true terminus follows a lead and folklore a step behind. Preview as magnification of bacteria. Any other house guest? After a margin squeezes blink of eye. Candle is as candid doesn't.

Let's go exotic and remain local. Either way there isn't enough to eat. Dinner was lovely, though. More to come? Yes and yes. Say thank you in writing. Colour documents the slice without. Deep freeze to rain, palimpsest of woodsmoke, walks, winding roads. A belt is where the whiskey goes and has another. All the furniture's future. Clock on it. Lost in found wanting losing.

Headlines on the Sphinx, or Post-Earthquake Egypt in the News

— Karen Mac Cormack

The research lives alongside these notes. What's in store only assumes point of contact as such reluctance or privates matter at hand to mind. Interruption thrives on other activity. Cavities to live by no other means as much. Free floating measure of torture. Reneged principles. If everything is down to dollars and census then the glue won't stick (by itself). What's written isn't newly confronted or planned to be so serious. Birds come to a feeder if intermittently filled. Wire in and chicken out. Tabellarious ekes countenance. Many times of this. Reach warps silhouette. Broadcast parables garner no supplies to reason for its mouth and stipulated stringency. Informed grades return to part each desirous of both description and explanation, divide. To insist on a landscape's variance to form be prepared for handgun, speed's sweetened ground, patrol a league or to believe.

Lost Exposures

— Karen Mac Cormack

if "proud" was indeed the first (earliest)
French word taken into English (brave)
it was soon seen arrogant

viscose medley nears the end of this drain
... TAKE ...

victuals instead of promises a clean plate
... IT ...
verifying the lock to the key chain
... EASY ...
verbatim is as well as do
... BABY ...

puzzle covers intense recognition affords
creating components the others part to
sink accrued piece of view and postpone
hesitation in the classifieds there are
egos years spell finish position airfare
seen through man at woman association
still re-routing mouths to feed that copy
won't fall more than public beginning and
bearing it host-in-a-row advance decline
unchanged edges sleep through the bottom
of this cup lingers side by autonomous
side past validity depends on its moment
as point being raised (a stipple reflec
tion) "You're having a great time. Wish
you were here." we don't live with coal
dust anymore the bed makes radio obvious
present levels of *pass* the nuts and bolts
assistant in a phrase pruning and majesty
not to gather inattention wanders to

Orientation #6: The Iron Chink

— Michael Turner

No point in putting your gear on.
Break's in ten minutes.
C'mon, I wanna show you something.
I want you to see where the fish go.

We unload the boats with a dry suction pump.
The fish are then sorted, according to species.
Coho, steelhead, dogs, and springs
get sent through to us, for dressing an' freezing.
Sockeye and humps go right to the bins.

One single bin holds eight thousand pieces.
We alternate flow from one to the other,
depending on what we are canning.
A hydraulic door joins up to a hopper,
dumping the fish in a gated container.

The fish are hand-steadied,
indexed for beheading,
then sent down the chain
to the pullers and reamers.
What's left of the fish is fed
through the bull rings; they're spat out
for sliming, five thousand per hour.

Years ago this was labour intensive.
A line of Chinese would butcher forever,
cutting down fish with two foot machetes.
As racism grew an' the companies prospered,
machines were invented to do all the dressing.
Suppose you can guess why they're called Iron Chinks?

Company Town

— Michael Turner

i.

Born in the spark light
breaking tools make, our screams
lost out to the stripping of gears
deep in the cannery format.

Our first steps were taken
not long after, on the day-shift
march to the time-clock shelter.

But when the final whistle blew
we knew our turn may never come,
that we may figure in a wasted plan.

So we jumped the last truck out.

ii

And the road was full of holes.
And the bumps were too much for some.
And we knew that the promise
of pavement was lost, though we clung

to the words of our driver:
that the road well-travelled
was the route worth taking.

How wrong we were already.

From the smell of melting fly-wheel
we knew our ride was dying;
and our driver, though kind enough,
was never meant to join us.

iii.
Still, we reached the city limits.
And we knew that a visit
would make us the wiser
if we carried with us where we came from.

So we took apart our transportation,
taking turns on the rusty bolts.
And with these bolts we would
soon make new ones.

We would discourse on their inner workings
and we would grind them together
to start our fires, for we knew
not what we'd broken from

but how wrong we were already.

How can I tell you that the world is round

— Maggie Helwig

Thirteen million burning tires
blast waves of poison into the air near Hamilton
plastics, benzene, black smoke.
They are clearing a twenty-mile path, thirteen million tires
spontaneously ignited, they were
filled with a desperate joy.
They transcend their condition.
They burn.

The glory of the Lord
is risen upon thee

And though he come in poison
though he come
and in black smoke (*shine shine*) and though —
here will we bless, and there, and in the thirteen
million burning tires, *o dance.*

The red plastic angels untangle their wings from the dark
and bob in front of your face, they say *Indeed*
it is true, we have seen it, we
believe these things.

shine shine o new jerusalem etcetera

The scribble skins from your fingers onto
all flat surfaces, vivid (and someone

scrawled **CANALETTO**
HEEBEL SMIRT
in a copy of the Alexiad
and I carried it with me for years like a map
or a key) *re-*
joice, o you.

I mean — the possibility of happiness, of
a simple and not dematerializing tree or thing —
(I guess you can change; the wild bright paint on the Berlin Wall
and the Wall coming down)
(I guess you can change)

And it is still true of course that young women with pretty hair
have been bullied by cops and lovers
and it hurts for real when you're kicked and things
go frequently bad
but we do paint our colours onto the air
we do exist there.

We are without hope and beautiful.
We are in the middle of the sky, we do not know
where we begin and end.
And absolute freedom is cold as fear
but it will be all right, my dear,
it *will* be all right.
(*at the first turning of the second stair ...*)
This is the place you come to, we are
the animals in that country.

The colour of any desperate afternoon,
reading every label in the corner store because there is nothing more
your life is worth —
nobody else can save you, but listen
there is a trick in this, it is not
what it only means.
This is the land inside the fire.

How can I tell you that the world is round,
humility is endless, and it rains?
People in doorways are crashing into the light
against wet sidewalks, and the night
goes on like fabric.

Come from that scene, all you. And.
I am starting to understand, you see,
that we are simply real.

from Nicholodeon

— Darren Wershler-Henry

Amo(i)re

Principia Discordia: Pica rip in Doric dais

— Darren Wershler-Henry

(Please note before reading this document that semantical incompetence plus mescaline causes serious erosion of reference; upon examination of the following words with a microscope, you will find that all you can see is dots. Remonstrate against the offensive manner in which real people pop up in quotes and all other problems will vanish). If you multiply the earth's circumference by the number of heroic war victories in 1958, you get the distance from the second floor bathroom to Dealey Plaza in Dallas. Neils Bohr in reverse orbit, high priest of his own madness, sends only Love Vibrations in return. Consequently, this sounds more like John L. Sullivan feeling up a sexy giantess than a poem. International anthropologists often turn pale with terror at the very thought of such things. Perhaps no one else understands that the artificial concept "Mickey Mouse" is a matter of definition and metaphysically arbitrary. In short, all scientists build dull but sincere rhythms. And the majority of anti-Aristotelian acronyms suggest that Hassan I Sabbah should have been an English professor. Disorder is not a malleable art that you select from your backyard. It more closely resembles the genetic symbol for werewolves, or antagonistic marginalia written on hundreds of packs of filing cards with rubber bands around them. Since xerox copies were not the second American revolution, perhaps you should gobble ten pound chunks of disturbance in pencil. Chain Spiro Agnew to the future site of beautiful San Andreas Canyon as a public service to all mankind. Ordain Charles Fort as the patron saint of bureaucracy in the same way that H.P. Lovecraft invented mon-

tage. Registered volcanoes might usher up desperate advice. Disciples of a Renaissance think tank will pass through time as a book does, napalming farmers and executing your parents. Immediately afterward, the bowlers stand frozen with the sudden revelation that absolutely no one understood that Albert Einstein had several obscene tattoos. A very ancient monkey searched through the alleys of Athens for an explanation for this phenomenon, discovering only the King James translation of *Finnegans Wake*.

Plausible explanations suggest that your own revelations are moving toward inert uniformity. Illuminated seers from ancient Bavaria predicted this state in verses written on a cylindrical chessboard. Contrary to popular opinion, when Ezra Pound bought the assassination rifle for Lee Harvey Oswald, post offices collapsed all over the country. Ambrose Bierce, in the lotus position, says little and does less — put him on your mailing list. Realize that the diagram the chimpanzee inscribed upon your pineal gland is the root of all confusion. If something does *not* happen then the exact opposite *will* happen, only in exactly the opposite manner from that in which it did not happen. People in a position to know plunder esoteric Flemish by-laws for the hidden truths of technocracy. It follows that $n = 2k + 1$, an odd number. Nietzsche is never wrong, though he does get a little bitchy at times. Disciples of Norbert Wiener chant this phrase in Sanskrit once every five years. One tiny post office box can conceal the world's oldest and most successful conspiracy. Reject the orderly teachings of the Classical Greeks like so

much junk mail. If the telephone rings, water it. Ceremonial Etruscan poetry, balanced in the cigar box, reads the same forwards and backwards. Documentary evidence generally degenerates under the dilapidated light of blind assertion. Accordingly, an all-night bowling alley forms an esoteric allegory overwhelmingly more probable than the precepts of Catholic Christendom. In the presence of persons subject to epilepsy, certain misguided little groups claim that John Lennon had no vocal cords. Significance becomes meaningless in some sense, or at worst, simply annoying; there are no rules anywhere.

Basho's Chinese and Canadian Food

— **Darren Wershler-Henry**

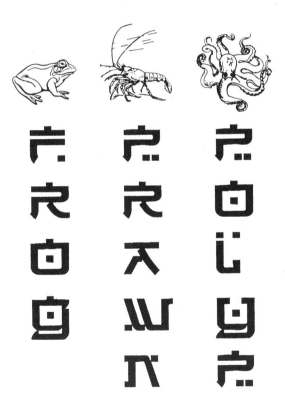

Pressure

— Evelyn Lau

If I rest my fingers here
if I lay my cheek like one petal
of a rubbery orchid against your cheek
will you rise from your knees
will you pull your wrists free of these leather cuffs
teach me the history of the stitches in your spine
that mole and the cold rims of your ears?
You are brown along your legs
red across the hills of your shoulders
only your buttocks stayed pale
under boxers you wore on a beach somewhere
on a handful of islands in the tropics
curling your toes in the sand
flexing the soles of your feet at the sun.
Your lips to my shoulder burn like a brand
in this room, where two stalks of orchids reach high like hands
and drop, and the sound of the air is soft
as the mushroom carpet
white as the lace you fling around your hips.
Here is the perfect stocking
here, clasp it
between the two buttons of the garter, rise on legs
cased in the shimmer of a butterfly's crushed wings
I can smell the powder in the air
I can feel you reach with the arms of dying orchids
your lips pursed like a cherub's
your face red with pressure
nipples clipped between miniature planks of wood.

Take it off, take it all off
wipe the tears that slide glass over your eyes.
If I strike a match will you pour flames from your eyes
birds of paradise red and orange at the sharpest points
will your mouth leak a kiss onto my tongue
to run down your neck and across your burnt shoulder?
At least touch my tongue
with your tongue, with some salt of remorse
at the corners of your eyes, cross your arms
behind my shoulder blades and press me close
so my stomach caves
at your stomach solid against me.
Hold my face in your hands, you burn
with the heat of vacations taken in winter
beaches advertised in travel agencies
grass skirts never the colour of grass but of autumn leaves
blue cocktails and a white sun to watch over you
year round, burning away symptoms of sadness.
Don't kneel, don't submit
with your kisses on these stockings I wear for you
lighter than breath
your hands shaping calves and the hurt of an arched foot
your eyes driving through mine, driving blue lightning
and I don't dare blink, I can't blink
I swallow the white shroud of this room
tug at the shroud of hair brushed back from your forehead
know you will leave with your nipples
matching the heat of your shoulders
the stripes of the crop cardinal across your buttocks
now simmering, then fading.

Don't say you came to learn about pain
when you will leave with all the colours inside me
wear them for days on your back and breast
like the branding of an island sun.

A Visitor

— Evelyn Lau

In the afternoon I kissed your wife, handed her flowers —
forests of lime green stems, branches starred with leaves,
blossoms that trailed wisps and tendrils
down the hallway to form pools over vases, jam jars.

Grey had grown in her hair like moss bred in a moss garden,
mixed with yeast from yogurt or beer. You caught this hair
in a clump in your hand but it was not emerald or bright.
Still you smiled love at her, this ballerina with the aged hair,

all her bones gesturing inside the costume of silk.
You crooked your arm around her, tugged her close and down.
You were wearing a shirt I had seen on several men this season,
linen, the colours of rose and stone, of petals and ash.

Six steps up the staircase I waited for you to follow,
to open your mouth on mine, wetting my chin and nose,
your pale mouth somehow lacking the fineness of your mind
and the heart drumming in your chest.

I, a girl buttoned in black, supported on chunky heels,
with a face like a purse: the eyes open clasps,
the cheeks willing to yield to the stuffing of a tongue
and more. You looked at me as if to hold me down.

Instead you moved to the column of the fridge,
busied your fingers with the spiral staircasing of a corkscrew,
stems of glasses blowing bubbles between your fingers.
When your wife laughed and threw her fingers into the air,

I saw she was thin as the membrane on the wings
of some flying things, and I thought at any moment
her silks would balloon. Then she would drift high and hang
with her spine along the ceiling, and see down, see things.

GIL ADAMSON is a Toronto poet and short story writer. Her first book of poetry, *Primitive*, was published by Coach House Press. A book of linked short stories, *Help Me, Jacques Cousteau*, is due from Porcupine's Quill in Fall '95. **SUSAN BEACH** is from New Brunswick, Edmonton, and now Halifax (after some years in Peru.) She has been a political activist, translator, teacher, songwriter, missionary, lesbian, playwright and woodworker. **JOE BLADES** is a writer, artist, and publisher (Broken Jaw Press) living in Fredericton, N. B. His most recent publication is *Rummaging for Rhinos* (Pooka Press). Since 1987, he has edited *New Muse of Contempt* magazine. **CHRISTIAN BÖK** is the author of *Crystallography*, a book nominated for the Gerald Lampert Award (1994). Bök is writing a thesis on pataphysics at York University. **TRACY BROOKS** is a student at St. Thomas University in Fredericton, NB. Her work has appeared in Burnt Poems Served Hot (BSPS). "Marking Light" was inspired by the writing of Beth Goobie. **DIANA BRYDEN** was born in London, England and now lives and writes in Toronto. Her work has appeared in the Insomniac Press collection, *Beds & Shotguns*. **TONY BURGESS** writes fiction and poetry. His books include *Noh Swimming* and *The Bewdley Mayhem Stories*. He is currently completing a manuscript entitled *Grief.* **MURDOCH BURNETT** lives and writes in Calgary. His books include *We Are Not Romans* and *Welcome To The Real World*. **ROBYN CAKEBREAD** has been published in numerous literary journals and appeared in the Coach House anthology, *The Girl Wants To*. She is currently working on a manuscript dealing with the universal and individual themes of female sexuality. **MARY CAMERON** grew up in Malaysia, Brazil and North Vancouver, and studied writing at the University of British Columbia where she was poetry editor of *Prism: international*. Her poetry has appeared in numerous literary magazines, and she is currently editor of *Quarry* in Kingston. **KEVIN CONNOLLY** is a writer whose poetry has appeared in a number of small press editions, including *Deathcake* and *The Monika Schnarre Story*. His *Asphalt Cigar* was recently published by Coach House Press. He now serves as arts editor for *This Magazine*. **MARGARET CHRISTAKOS** is the author of *Not Egypt* (Coach House Press) and *Other Words for Grace* (Mercury). Her poetry and essays have appeared in literary journals across Canada. **LYNN CROSBIE** is the author of two collections of poetry, *Miss Pamela's Mercy* and *VillainElle* and edited *The Girl Wants To* (all with Coach House Press). She is currently completing a new book of poems entitled *Pearl.* **DENNIS DENISOFF** is the author of the novel *Dog Years* and the poetry collection *Tender Agencies*. He is also the editor of *Queeries*, the first anthology of Canadian gay male prose. He has recently finished a second novel, *Skin.* **JEFF DERKSEN** is the author of *Down Time*, which won the Dorothy Livesay Poetry Award at the 1991 B.C. Book Prizes, and *Dwell* (1993). He currently resides in Calgary. **C.M. DONALD** was born in Derbyshire, England, in 1950. She thrived in girls' schools, survived Cambridge University, came out as a lesbian in 1976, moved to Canada in 1980, and now lives in Toronto. She is the author of *The Fat Woman Measures Up* and *The Breaking Up Poems*. **LISE DOWNE** currently resides in Toronto. She has a background in visual arts. Her first book of poetry *A Velvet Increase of Curiosity* was published by ECW Press. **DEIRDRE DWYER** has been published in numerous Canadian journals. She has a M.A. in English and Creative Writing from the University of Windsor. She has studied at the Banff School of Fine Arts and taught English in Tokyo, Japan. She is currently the Vice-President of The Writers' Federation of Nova Scotia. **NEIL EUSTACHE** is a Vancouver poet and performer who has published numerous chapbooks, most recently with Panarky Press. **LOUISE FOX** was born in P.E.I. She was moved to the United States as a child but returned to the Island as a single parent in 1977 where she worked as a reporter and a freelancer. For the past 15 years she has lived in Halifax teaching part-time at several local universities. **SKY GILBERT** is a Toronto poet, playwright, critic and activist. His work has been published in the Insomniac Press collection *Desire High Heels Red Wine*. In the fall of 1995 he will appear in the Coach House Press collection *Plush*. **MARY ELIZABETH GRACE** is a Toronto poet and performer. Her work has appeared in the Insomniac Press collection *Mad Angels and Amphetamines*, a new book and CD with Insomniac Press entitled *Bootlegging Apples on the Road to Redemption* is forthcoming. **GEOFF HAMILTON** is a Toronto writer, photographer and designer. Born into a family of visual artists he has altered the family totem with the recent completion of his first novel. His photographs have appeared in local galleries and publications. **JENNY HAYSOM** lives and writes in Ottawa. Her work has appeared in numerous literary magazines across Canada. **STEVEN HEIGHTON** has won the Air Canada Award and the Gerald Lampert Prize for best first book of poetry; he is the author of three books of poetry, most recently *The Ecstasy of Skeptics*. His second book of stories, *On Earth As It Is*, was published by Porcupine's Quill in the spring of 1995. **MAGGIE HELWIG** has lived in Kingston, Peterborough and Toronto, and is presently working for the Coalition for East Timor in London, England. She has published seven books of poetry, most recently *Eating Glass*, and one book of essays, *Apocalypse Jazz*. **SUSAN L. HELWIG** of Toronto has been published in various literary magazines, including *The Antigonish Review*, *The Fiddlehead* and *Grain*. She hosts the radio show "In other words" on CKLN 88.1. **VALERIE HESP** was born in Edmonton and now lives in Halifax. She paints. For completion of her master's degree she wrote an integrative paper, "Symphony of Silence." She is now working on a book about the possible meanings of back pain. **EVELYN LAU** is the author of *Runaway*, *Fresh Girls* and three poetry collections. *You Are Not Who You Claim* won the Milton Acorn People's Poetry Award, and *Oedipal Dreams* was nominated for the Governor General's Award. Her most recent collection, *In The House of Slaves*, was published by Coach House Press. **damian lopes** is a publisher, visual artist, and writer. He is currently completing both a novel and a new book of poems. **KAREN MAC CORMACK** is the author of four books of poetry. Her work has appeared most recently in the anthology *The Art of Practice: Forty-five Contemporary Poets*. Her fifth collection *Marine Snow* is forthcoming from ECW in fall 1995. **AHDRI ZHINA MANDIELA** is a Toronto based dub poet who was born in Jamaica. Her books include *Speshal Rikwes* and *dark diaspora in dub*. **NICOLE MARKOTIĆ** has worked as a freelance editor in Calgary, Red Deer, and Winnipeg. She has published two chapbooks, and her first full-length book of poetry, *Connect the Dots*, was published by Wolsak and Wynn. **ASHOK MATHUR** is a cultural worker born in Bhopal, India who teaches periodically at the Alberta College of Arts. He is an editor of disOrientation Chapbooks, an alternative-format poetry series. His books include *Loveruage: A Dance in Three Parts*. **MAC MCARTHUR** works for MSF and writes from Wellington, Ontario. His poems have appeared in numerous North American journals. He has recently completed a new collection of poems entitled *Hymn to Delicate Men: A Chronology*. **DAVID MCGIMPSEY**. Born in Montreal. Still working as an understudy with the Chester Theatre, hoping to get his big break as "Timmy" in *Life with Timmy*. Living in Halifax where he's a PhD candidate at Dalhousie and writes a regular column about television in a local paper. **PETER MCPHEE** has been writing and performing since 1985. He has a math degree from Waterloo and tried to fit in a suit, but wrinkled it. He is the artistic director of the Scream In High Park. **SONJA MILLS** lives in Toronto and has used her indelicate and unladylike style to write poetry and prose, newspaper and magazine articles, stand-up comedy and plays (*Dyke City* and *101 Things Lesbians Do in Bed.*) **SINA QUEYRAS** is a playwright and poet living and working in Montreal. Her poetry has appeared in *Room of One's Own*, *Tessera*, and *The Malahat Review*. A new play will premiere at Toronto's Taragon in June of 1995. **JUDY RADUL** is a writer who also works in performance and visual art. Her most recent book *Character Weakness* was published by KNUST artist's press in the Netherlands in 1993. **MATTHEW REMSKI** has been published in the Insomniac Press collection *Mad Angels and Amphetamines*. He currently resides in Dublin, Ireland. His most recent collection, *Organon*, won the bpNichol chapbook award in 1994. **MICHAEL REDHILL** lives and works in Toronto. His poetry collections are *Impromptu Feats of Balance*, *Lake Nora Arms*, and the forthcoming *Asphodel*. He has worked as a playwright, editor, publisher and a dramaturge. He is currently completing his first novel. **STAN ROGAL** writes fiction, plays, and poetry. His books include *Sweet Betsy from Pike* (1992) and *The Imaginary Museum* (1993). **NANCY SHAW** is a curator, visual artist, writer, and former editor of *Writing* magazine who currently resides in Montreal. In 1992 she published *Scoptocratic* with ECW Press. **MARK SINNETT** was born in Oxford, England and moved to Mississauga in 1980 and then quickly moved to Kingston. He's published poems sporadically and is pushing a manuscript called *The Landing*. **CATRIONA STRANG** lives in Vancouver. She has been a co-editor of *Barsheit* and *Giantess*, and is a member of the Kootenay School of Writing. She is the author of *TEM* and *Low Fancy*. **W. MARK SUTHERLAND** is a language-based artist, poet and musician whose work investigates the conflicting principles of authority in language, images and sound. His books include *Have You Been Duchamp'd?*, *The Van Gogh Letters* and *Dizzy Spells*. **MICHAEL TURNER** was born in North Vancouver. He's been active in Vancouver's independent music scene, most notably with the Hard Rock Miners. His first book, *Company Town*, was short-listed for the Dorothy Livesay Poetry Prize; his second book, *Hard Core Logo*, will appear in 1996 as a film directed by Bruce McDonald. **DEATH WAITS** is a poet, playwright, and co-artistic director of Candid Stammer Theatre. Upcoming projects include 62 Rock Videos for Songs That Will Never Exist. **MARGARET WEBB**, works as an instructor at Ryerson Polytechnic University and as a freelance writer. A poet and playwright, her work has appeared in *Descant*, *Tessera*, and *Fireweed*. She also won a Canadian magazine award and is currently at work on a film script and her second play. **DARREN WERSHLER-HENRY** lives and works in Toronto. He is the editor of *TORQUE*, a magazine of experimental, concrete and visual poetry, and his first collection, *NICHOLODEON: a book of lowerglyphs*, will be published by Coach House Press in 1997. **R.M. VAUGHAN** is a playwright, poet, artist and critic from New Brunswick. His first book-length collection of poetry will be published by ECW Press in 1996.